A MONSTER HELPING OF
HORRID HENRY

Francesca Simon spent her childhood on the beach
in California, and then went to Yale and Oxford
Universities to study medieval history and literature.
She now lives in London with her family. She has
written over fifty books and won the Children's Book
of the Year in 2008 at the Galaxy British Book Awards
for *Horrid Henry and the Abominable Snowman*.

Tony Ross is one of Britain's best-known illustrators,
with many picture books to his name as well as line
drawings for many fiction titles. He lives in Powys.

D0400888

Also by Francesca Simon

Don't Cook Cinderella
Helping Hercules

and for younger readers

The Topsy-Turvies
Illustrated by Emily Bolam

Spider School
Illustrated by Tony Ross

Café at the Edge of the Moon
The Parent Swap Shop
Mr P's Naughty Book
Illustrated by Pete Williamson

There are many **Horrid Henry** books available.
For a complete list visit **www.horridhenry.co.uk** or
www.orionbooks.co.uk

A MONSTER
HELPING OF
HORRID HENRY

Francesca Simon
Illustrated by Tony Ross

Orion
Children's Books

This collection first published in Great Britain in 2013
by Orion Children's Books
a division of the Orion Publishing Group Ltd
Orion House
5 Upper St Martin's Lane
London WC2H 9EA
An Hachette UK Company

5 7 9 10 8 6

The Orion Publishing Group's policy is to use papers that are natural,
renewable and recyclable products and made from wood grown in sustainable
forests. The logging and manufacturing processes are expected to conform to
the environmental regulations of the country of origin.

A catalogue record for this book is available from the British Library.

ISBN 978 1 4440 0923 1

Printed in Great Britain by Clays Ltd, St Ives plc

www.horridhenry.co.uk
www.orionbooks.co.uk

CONTENTS

1

HORRID HENRY'S INVASION

'Baa! Baa! Baa!'

Perfect Peter baaed happily at his sheep collection. There they were, his ten lovely little sheepies, all beautifully lined up from biggest to smallest, heads facing forward, fluffy tails against the wall, all five centimetres apart from one another, all—

Perfect Peter gasped. Something was wrong. Something was terribly wrong. But what? What? Peter scanned the mantelpiece. Then he saw . . .

Nooooo!

Fluff Puff, his favourite sheep, the one with the pink and yellow nose, was facing the wrong way round. His nose was shoved against the wall. His tail was facing forward. And he was . . . he was . . . crooked!

This could only mean . . . this could only mean . . .

'Mum!' screamed Peter. 'Mum! Henry's been in my room again!'

'Henry!' shouted Mum. 'Keep out of Peter's room.'

'I'm not in Peter's room,' yelled Horrid Henry. 'I'm in mine.'

'But he was,' wailed Peter.

'Wasn't!' bellowed Horrid Henry.

Tee hee.

Horrid Henry was strictly forbidden to go into Peter's bedroom without Peter's permission. But sometimes, thought Horrid Henry, when Peter was being

12

even more of a toady toad than usual, he had no choice but to invade.

Peter had run blabbing to Mum that Henry had watched *Mutant Max* and *Knight Fight* when Mum had said he could only watch one or the other. Henry had been banned from watching TV all day. Peter was such a telltale frogface ninnyhammer toady poo bag, thought Horrid Henry grimly. Well, just wait till Peter tried to colour in his new picture, he'd—

'MUM!' screamed Peter. 'Henry switched the caps on my coloured pens. I just put pink in the sky.'

'Didn't!' yelled Henry.

'Did!' wailed Peter.

'Prove it,' said Horrid Henry, smirking.

Mum came upstairs. Quickly Henry leapt over the mess covering the floor of his room, flopped on his bed and grabbed a *Screamin' Demon* comic. Peter came and stood in the doorway.

'Henry's being horrid,' snivelled Peter.

'Henry, have you been in Peter's room?' said Mum.

Henry sighed loudly. 'Of course I've been in his smelly room. I live here, don't I?'

'I mean when he wasn't there,' said Mum.

'No,' said Horrid Henry. This wasn't a lie, because even if Peter *wasn't* there his horrible stinky smell was.

'He has too,' said Peter. 'Fluff Puff was turned the wrong way round.'

'Maybe he was just trying to escape from your pongy pants,' said Henry. '*I* would.'

'Mum!' said Peter.

'Henry! Don't be horrid. Leave your brother alone.'

'I *am* leaving him alone,' said Horrid Henry. 'Why can't he leave *me* alone? And get out of *my* room, Peter!' he shrieked, as Peter put his foot just inside Henry's door.

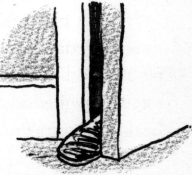

Peter quickly withdrew his foot.

Henry glared at Peter.

Peter glared at Henry.

Mum sighed. 'The next one who goes into the other's room without permission will be banned from the computer for a week. And no pocket money either.'

She turned to go.

Henry stuck out his tongue at Peter.

'Telltale,' he mouthed.

'Mum!' screamed Peter.

Perfect Peter stalked back to his bedroom. How dare Henry sneak in and mess up his sheep? What a mean, horrible brother. Perhaps he needed to calm down and listen to a little music. The *Daffy and her Dancing Daisies Greatest Hits* CD always cheered him up.

'Dance and prance. Prance and dance.

You say moo moo. We say baa.

Everybody says moo moo baa baa,'
piped Perfect Peter as he put on the
Daffy CD.

**Boils on your fat face
Boils make you dumb.
Chop Chop Chop 'em off
Stick 'em on your bum!**

blared the CD player.

Huh? What was that horrible song?
Peter yanked out the CD. It was the
Skullbangers singing the horrible 'Bony
Boil' song. Henry must have sneaked a
Skullbanger CD inside the Daffy case.
How dare he? How dare he? Peter
would storm straight downstairs and
tell Mum. Henry would get into big
trouble. Big big trouble.

Then Peter paused. There *was* the
teeny-tiny possibility that Peter had

mixed them up by mistake . . . No.
He needed absolute proof of Henry's
horridness. He'd do his homework, then
have a good look around Henry's room
to see if his Daffy CD was hidden there.

Peter glanced at his 'To Do' list
pinned on his noticeboard. When he'd
written it that morning it read:

Peter's To Do List
Practise cello
Fold clothes and put away
Do homework
Brush my teeth
Read Bunny's Big Boo Boo

The list now read:

Peter's To Do List
Practise ~~cello~~ belly dancing
unFold clothes and ~~Put~~ away
~~throw~~
Don't ~~Do~~ do homework
~~Flush~~ my teeth ~~down the toilet~~
Read Bunny's Big ~~Poo~~ Poo

At the bottom someone had added:

Pick my nose
Pinch mum
Give Henry all my money

Well, here was proof! He was going to go straight down and tell on Henry.

'Mum! Henry's been in my room again. He scribbled all over my To Do list.'

'Henry!' screamed Mum. 'I am sick and tired of this! Keep out of your brother's bedroom! This is your last warning! No playing on the computer for a week!'

Sneak. Sneak. Sneak.

Horrid Henry slipped inside the enemy's bedroom. He'd pay Peter back for getting him banned from the computer.

There was Peter's cello. Ha! It was the work of a moment to unwind all the strings. Now, what else, what else? He could switch around Peter's pants and sock drawers.

No! Even better. Quickly Henry undid all of Peter's socks, and mismatched them. Who said socks should match?

Tee hee. Peter would go mad when he found out he was wearing one Sammy the Snail sock with one Daffy sock. Then Henry snatched Bunnykins off Peter's bed and crept out.

Sneak. Sneak. Sneak.

Perfect Peter crept down the hall and stood outside Henry's bedroom, holding a muddy twig. His heart was pounding. Peter knew he was strictly forbidden to go into Henry's room without permission. But Henry kept breaking that rule. So why shouldn't he?

Squaring his shoulders, Peter tiptoed in.

Crunch.

Crunch.

Crunch.

Henry's room was a pigsty, thought Perfect Peter, wading through broken knights, crumpled sweet wrappers, dirty clothes, ripped comics, and muddy shoes.

Mr Kill. He'd steal Mr Kill. Ha! Serve Henry right. And he'd put the muddy twig in Henry's bed. Serve him double right. Perfect Peter grabbed Mr Kill, shoved the twig in Henry's bed and nipped back to his room.

And screamed.

Fluff Puff wasn't just turned the wrong way, he was – gone! Henry must have stolen him. And Lambykins was

gone too. And Squish. Peter only had seven sheep left. 🐑 🐑 🐑 🐑 🐑 🐑 🐑

And where was his Bunnykins? He wasn't on the bed where he belonged. No!!!!!! This was the last straw. This was war.

The coast was clear. Peter always took ages having his bath. Horrid Henry slipped into the worm's room.

He'd pay Peter back for stealing Mr
Kill. There he was, shoved at the top of
Peter's wardrobe, where Peter always
hid things he didn't want Henry to find.
Well, ha ha ha, thought Horrid Henry,
rescuing Mr Kill.

Now what to do, what to do?
Horrid Henry scooped up all of Peter's
remaining sheep and shoved them inside
Peter's pillowcase.

What else? Henry glanced round Peter's immaculate room. He could mess it up. Nah, thought Henry. Peter loved tidying. He could – aha.

Peter had pinned drawings all over the wall above his bed. Henry surveyed them. Shame, thought Henry, that Peter's pictures were all so dull. I mean, really, 'My Family', and 'My Bunnykins'. Horrid Henry climbed on Peter's bed to reach the drawings.

Poor Peter, thought Horrid Henry. What a terrible artist he was. No wonder he was such a smelly toad if he had to look at such awful pictures all the time. Perhaps Henry could improve them . . .

Now, let's see, thought Horrid Henry, getting out some crayons. Drawing a crown on my head would be a big improvement. There! That livens things up. And a big red nose on Peter would help, too, thought Henry, drawing away. So would a droopy moustache on Mum. And as for that stupid picture of Bunnykins, well, why not draw a lovely toilet for him to—

'What are you doing in here?' came a little voice.

Horrid Henry turned.

There was Peter, in his bunny pyjamas, glaring at him.

Uh oh. If Peter told on him again, Henry would be in big, big, mega-big trouble. Mum would probably ban him from the computer for ever.

'You're in my room. I'm telling on you,' shrieked Peter.

'Shhh!' hissed Horrid Henry.

'What do you mean, shhh?' said

Peter. 'I'm going straight down to tell Mum.'

'One word and you're dead, worm,' said Horrid Henry. 'Quick! Close the door.'

Perfect Peter looked behind him. 'Why?'

'Just do it, worm,' hissed Henry.

Perfect Peter shut the door.

'What are you doing?' he demanded.

'Dusting for fingerprints,' said Horrid Henry smoothly.

Fingerprints?

'What?' said Peter.

'I thought I heard someone in your room, and ran in to check you were okay. Just look what I found,' said Horrid Henry dramatically, pointing to Peter's now empty mantelpiece.

Peter let out a squeal.

'My sheepies!' wailed Peter.

'I think there's a burglar in the
house,' whispered Horrid Henry
urgently. 'And I think he's hiding . . .
in your room.'

Peter gulped. A burglar? In his room?

'A burglar?'

'Too right,' said Henry. 'Who do you
think stole Bunnykins? And all your
sheep?'

'You,' said Peter.

Horrid Henry snorted. 'No! What
would I want with your stupid sheep?

28

But a sheep rustler would love them.'

Perfect Peter hesitated. Could Henry be telling the truth? *Could* a burglar really have stolen his sheep?

'I think he's hiding under the bed,' hissed Horrid Henry. 'Why don't you check?'

Peter stepped back.

'No,' said Peter. 'I'm scared.'

'Then get out of here as quick as you can,' whispered Henry. '*I'll* check.'

'Thank you, Henry,' said Peter.

Perfect Peter crept into the hallway. Then he stopped. Something wasn't right . . . something was a little bit wrong.

Perfect Peter marched back into his bedroom. Henry was by the door.

'I think the burglar is hiding in your wardrobe, I'll get—'

'You said you were fingerprinting,' said Peter suspiciously. 'With what?'

'My fingers,' said Horrid Henry. 'Why do you think it's called *finger*printing?'

Then Peter caught sight of his drawings.

'You've ruined my pictures!' shrieked Peter.

'It wasn't me, it must have been the burglar,' said Horrid Henry.

'You're trying to trick me,' said Peter.

'I'm telling!'

Time for Plan B.

'I'm only in here 'cause you were in my room,' said Henry.

'Wasn't!'

'Were!'

'Liar!'

31

'Liar!'

'You stole Bunnykins!'

'You stole Mr Kill!'

'Thief!'

'Thief!'

'I'm telling on you.'

'I'm telling on you!'

Henry and Peter glared at each other.

'Okay,' said Horrid Henry. 'I won't invade your room if you won't invade mine.'

'Okay,' said Perfect Peter. He'd agree to anything to get Henry to leave his sheep alone.

Horrid Henry smirked.

He couldn't wait until tomorrow when Peter tried to play his cello . . . tee hee.

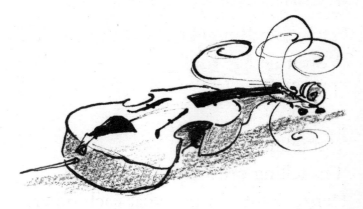

Wouldn't he get a shock!

2

MOODY MARGARET'S SLEEPOVER

'What are you doing here?' said Moody Margaret, glaring.

'I'm here for the sleepover,' said Sour Susan, glaring back.

'You were uninvited, remember?' said Margaret.

'And then you invited me again, remember?' snapped Susan.

'Did not.'

'Did too. You told me last week I could come.'

'Didn't.'

'Did. You're such a meanie,
Margaret,' scowled Susan. Aaaarrggghh.
Why was she friends with such a
moody old grouch?

Moody Margaret heaved a heavy sigh.
Why was she friends with such a sour
old slop bucket?

'Well, since you're here, I guess you'd
better come in,' said Margaret. 'But
don't expect any dessert 'cause there
won't be enough for you and my *real*
guests.'

Sour Susan stomped inside Margaret's
house. Grrrr. She wouldn't be inviting
Margaret to her next sleepover party,
that's for sure.

Horrid Henry couldn't sleep. He was
hot. He was hungry.

'Biscuits!' moaned his tummy. 'Give
me biscuits!'

Because Mum
and Dad were
the meanest,
most horrible
parents in the
world, they'd
forgotten to buy
more biscuits
and there wasn't a single solitary crumb
in the house. Henry knew because he'd
searched everywhere.

'Give me biscuits!' growled his
tummy. 'What are you waiting for?'

I'm going to die of hunger up here,
thought Horrid Henry. And it will be
all Mum and Dad's fault. They'll come
in tomorrow morning and find just a
few wisps of hair and some teeth. Then
they'd be sorry. Then they'd wail and
gnash. But it would be too late.

'How could we have forgotten to buy

chocolate biscuits?' Dad would sob.

'We deserve to be locked up forever!' Mum would shriek.

'And now there's nothing left of Henry but a tooth, and it's all our fault!' they'd howl.

Humph. Serve them right.

Wait. What an idiot he was. Why should he risk death from starvation when he knew where there was a rich stash of all sorts of yummy biscuits waiting just for him?

Moody Margaret's Secret Club tent was sure to be full to bursting with

goodies! Horrid Henry hadn't raided it
in ages. And so long as he was quick,
no one would ever know he'd left the
house.

'Go on, Henry,' urged his tummy.
'FEED ME!'

Horrid Henry
didn't need to
be urged twice.

Slowly,
quietly, he
sneaked out of
bed, crept down
the stairs, and tiptoed out of the back
door. Then quick over the wall, and
hey presto, he was in the Secret Club
tent. There was Margaret's Secret Club
biscuit tin, in her pathetic hiding place
under a blanket. Ha!

Horrid Henry prised open the lid.
Oh wow. It was filled to the brim with

Chocolate Fudge Chewies! And those
scrumptious Triple Chocolate Chip
Marshmallow Squidgies! Henry scooped
up a huge handful and stuffed them in
his mouth.

Chomp. Chomp. Chomp.

Oh wow. Oh wow. Was there
anything more delicious in the whole
wide world than a mouthful of nicked
biscuits?

'More! More! More!' yelped his
tummy.

Who was Horrid Henry to say no?

Henry reached in to snatch another mega handful . . .

BANG! SLAM! BANG!

STOMP! STOMP! STOMP!

'That's too bad, Gurinder,' snapped Margaret's voice. 'It's my party so I decide. Hurry up, Susan.'

'I am hurrying,' said Susan's voice.

The footsteps were heading straight for the Secret Club tent.

Yikes. What was Margaret doing outside at this time of night? There wasn't a moment to lose.

Horrid Henry looked around wildly. Where could he hide? There was a wicker chest at the back, where Margaret kept her dressing-up clothes. Horrid Henry leapt inside and pulled the lid shut. Hopefully, the girls wouldn't be long and he could escape

home before Mum and Dad discovered he'd been out.

Moody Margaret bustled into the tent, followed by her mother, Gorgeous Gurinder, Kung-Fu Kate, Lazy Linda, Vain Violet, Singing Soraya and Sour Susan.

'Now, girls, it's late, I want you to go straight to bed, lights out, no talking,' said Margaret's mother. 'My little Maggie Moo Moo needs her beauty sleep.'

42

Ha, thought Horrid Henry. Margaret could sleep for a thousand years and she'd still look like a frog.

'Yes, Mum,' said Margaret.

'Good night, girls,' trilled Margaret's mum. 'See you in the morning.'

Phew, thought Horrid Henry, lying as still as he could. He'd be back home in no time, mission safely accomplished.

'We're sleeping out here?' said Singing Soraya. 'In a tent?'

'I said it was a Secret Club sleepover,' said Margaret.

Horrid Henry's heart sank. Huh?
They were planning to sleep here? Rats
rats rats double rats. He was going to
have to hide inside this hot dusty chest
until they were asleep.

Maybe they'd all fall asleep soon,
thought Horrid Henry hopefully.

Because he had to get home before
Mum and Dad discovered he was
missing. If they realised he'd sneaked
outside, he'd be in so much trouble
his life wouldn't be worth living and
he might as well abandon all hope of
ever watching TV or eating another
biscuit until he was an old, shrivelled
bag of bones struggling to chew with
his one tooth and watch telly with his
magnifying glass and hearing aid. Yikes!

Horrid Henry looked grimly at the
biscuits clutched in his fist. Thank
goodness he'd brought provisions. He

might be trapped here for a very long
time.

'Where's your sleeping bag, Violet?'
said Margaret.

'I didn't bring one,' said Vain Violet.
'I don't like sleeping on the floor.'

'Tough,' said Margaret, 'that's where
we're sleeping.'

'But I need to sleep in a bed,' whined
Vain Violet. 'I don't want to sleep out
here.'

'Well we do,' said Margaret.

'Yeah,' said Susan.

'I can sleep anywhere,' said Lazy Linda, yawning.

'I'm calling my mum,' said Violet. 'I want to go home.'

'Go ahead,' said Margaret. 'We don't need you, do we?'

Silence.

'Oh go on, Violet, stay,' said Gurinder.

'Yeah, stay,' said Kung-Fu Kate.

'No!' said Violet, flouncing out of the tent.

'Hummph,' said Moody Margaret.

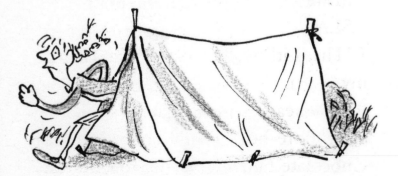

'She's no fun anyway. Now, everyone put your sleeping bags down where I say. I need to sleep by the entrance, because I need fresh air.'

'I want to sleep by the entrance,' said Soraya.

'No,' said Margaret, 'it's my party so I decide. Susan, you go at the back because you snore.'

'Do not,' said Susan.

'Do too,' said Margaret.

'Liar.'

'Liar.'

SLAP!

SLAP!

'That's it!' wailed Susan. 'I'm calling my mum.'

'Go ahead,' said Margaret, 'see if I care, snore-box. That'll be loads more Chocolate Fudge Chewies for the rest of us.'

Sour Susan stood still. She'd been looking forward to Margaret's sleepover for ages. And she still hadn't had any of the midnight feast Margaret had promised.

'All right, I'll stay,' said Susan sourly, putting her sleeping bag down at the back of the tent by the dressing-up chest.

'I want to be next to Gurinder,' said Lazy Linda, scratching her head.

'Do you have nits?' said Gurinder.

'No!' said Linda.

'You do too,' said Gurinder.

'Do not,' said Linda.

'Do too,' said Gurinder. 'I'm not sleeping next to someone who has nits.'

'Me neither,' said Kate.

'Me neither,' said Soraya.

'Don't look at me,' said Margaret. 'I'm not sleeping next to you.'

'I don't have nits!' wailed Linda.

'Go next to Susan,' said Margaret.

'But she snores,' protested Linda.

'But she has nits,' protested Susan.

'Do not.'

'Do not.'

'Nitty!'

'Snory!'

Suddenly something scuttled across the floor.

'EEEEK!' squealed Soraya. 'It's

a mouse!' She scrambled onto the
dressing-up chest. The lid sagged.

'It won't hurt you,' said Margaret.

'Yeah,' said Susan.

'Eeeek!' squealed Linda, shrinking
back.

The lid sagged even more.

Cree—eaaak went the chest.

Aaarrrrggghhh, thought Horrid
Henry, trying to squash himself down
before he was squished.

'Eeeek!' squealed Gurinder,
scrambling onto the chest.

CREE—EAAAAAK! went the chest.

Errrrgh, thought Horrid Henry,
pushing up against the sagging lid as
hard as he could.

'I can't sleep if there's a . . . mouse,'
said Gurinder. She looked around
nervously. 'What if it runs on top of my
sleeping bag?'

Margaret sighed. 'It's only a mouse,' she said.

'I'm scared of mice,' whimpered Gurinder. 'I'm leaving!' And she ran out of the tent, wailing.

'More food for the rest of us,' said Margaret, shrugging. 'I say we feast now.'

'About time,' said Soraya.

'Let's start with the Chocolate Fudge Chewies,' said Margaret, opening the

51

Secret Club biscuit tin. 'Everyone can have two, except for me, I get four 'cause it's my . . .'

Margaret peered into the tin. There were only a few crumbs inside.

'Who stole the biscuits?' said Margaret.

'Wasn't me,' said Susan.

'Wasn't me,' said Soraya.

'Wasn't me,' said Kate.

'Wasn't me,' said Linda.

Tee hee, thought Horrid Henry.

'One of you did, so no one is getting anything to eat until you admit it,' snapped Margaret.

'Meanie,' muttered Susan sourly.

'What did you say?' said Moody Margaret.

'Nothing,' said Susan.

'Then we'll just have to wait for the culprit to come forward,' said Margaret, scowling. 'Meanwhile, get in your sleeping bags. We're going to tell scary stories in the dark. Who knows a good one?'

'I do,' said Susan.

'Not the story about the ghost kitty-cat which drank up all the milk in your kitchen, is it?' said Margaret.

Susan scowled.

'Well, it's a true scary story,' said Susan.

'I know a real scary story,' said Kung-Fu Kate. 'It's about this monster—'

'Mine's better,' said Margaret. 'It's about a flesh-eating zombie which creeps around at night and rips off—'

'NOOOO,' wailed Linda. 'I hate being scared. I'm calling my mum to come and get me.'

'No scaredy-cats allowed in the Secret Club,' said Margaret.

'I don't care,' said Linda, flouncing out.

'It's not a sleepover unless we tell ghost stories,' said Moody Margaret. 'Turn off your torches. It won't be scary unless we're all sitting in the dark.'

Sniffle. Sniffle. Sniffle.

'I want to go home,' snivelled Soraya.

'I've never slept away from home before . . . I want my mummy.'

'What a baby,' said Moody Margaret.

Horrid Henry was cramped and hot and uncomfortable. Pins and needles were shooting up his arm. He shifted his shoulder, brushing against the lid.

There was a muffled creak.

Henry froze. Whoops. Henry prayed they hadn't heard anything.

'. . . and the zombie crept inside the tent gnashing its bloody teeth and sniffing the air for human flesh, hungry for more—'

Ow. His poor aching arm. Henry shifted position again.

Creak . . .

'What was that?' whispered Susan.

'What was what?' said Margaret.

'There was a . . . a . . . creak . . .' said

Susan.

'The wind,' said Margaret. 'Anyway, the zombie sneaked into the tent and—'

'You don't think . . .' hissed Kate.

'Think what?' said Margaret.

'That the zombie . . . the zombie . . .'

I'm starving, thought Horrid Henry. I'll just eat a few biscuits really, really, really quietly—

Crunch. Crunch.

'What was that?' whispered Susan.

'What was what?' said Margaret. 'You're ruining the story.'

'That . . . crunching sound,' hissed Susan.

Horrid Henry gasped. What an idiot he was! Why hadn't he thought of this before?

Crunch. Crunch. Crunch.

'Like someone . . . someone . . . crunching on . . . bones,' whispered Kung-Fu Kate.

'Someone . . . here . . .' whispered Susan.

Tap. Horrid Henry rapped on the underside of the lid.

Tap! Tap! Tap!

'I didn't hear anything,' said Margaret loudly.

'It's the zombie!' screamed Susan.

'He's in here!' screamed Kate. 'AAAAARRRRRRRGHHHHHHH!'

'I'm going home!' screamed Susan and Kate. 'MUMMMMMMMMMYYYY!' they wailed, running off.

Ha ha, thought Horrid Henry. His brilliant plan had worked!!! Tee hee. He'd hop out, steal the rest of the feast and scoot home. Hopefully Mum and Dad—

YANK!

Suddenly the chest lid was flung open and a torch shone in his eyes. Moody

Margaret's hideous face glared down at him.

'Gotcha!' said Moody Margaret. 'Oh boy, are you in trouble. Just wait till I tell on you. Ha ha, Henry, you're dead.'

Horrid Henry climbed out of the chest and brushed a few crumbs onto the carpet.

'Just wait till I tell everyone at school about your sleepover,' said Horrid Henry. 'How you were so mean and bossy everyone ran away.'

'Your parents will punish you forever,' said Moody Margaret.

'Your name will be mud forever,' said Horrid Henry. 'Everyone will laugh at you and serves you right, Maggie Moo Moo.'

'Don't call me that,' said Margaret, glaring.

'Call you what, Moo Moo?'

'All right,' said Margaret slowly. 'I won't tell on you if you give me two packs of Chocolate Fudge Chewies.'

'No way,' said Henry. 'I won't tell on you if you give me three packs of Chocolate Fudge Chewies.'

'Fine,' said Margaret. 'Your parents are still up, I'll tell them where you are right now. I wouldn't want them to worry.'

'Go ahead,' said Henry. 'I can't wait until school tomorrow.'

Margaret scowled.

'Just this once,' said Horrid Henry. 'I won't tell on you if you won't tell on me.'

'Just this once,' said Moody Margaret. 'But never again.'

They glared at each other.

When he was king, thought Horrid

Henry, anyone named Margaret would be catapulted over the walls into an oozy swamp. Meanwhile . . . on guard, Margaret. On guard. I will be avenged!

3

HORRID HENRY'S AUTOBIOGRAPHY

Bang! Crash! Kaboom!

Rude Ralph bounced on a chair and did his Tarzan impression.

Moody Margaret yanked Lazy Linda's hair. Linda screamed.

Stone-Age Steven stomped round the room grunting 'Ugg.'

'Rat about town
don't need a gown.
where I'm goin'
Only fangs'll be Showin,'

shrieked Horrid Henry.

'Quiet!' barked Miss Battle-Axe.

'Settle down immediately.'

Ralph bounced.

Steven stomped.

Linda screamed.

Henry shrieked. He was the Killer Boy Rats new lead singer, blasting his music into the roaring crowd, hurling—

'HENRY, BE QUIET!' bellowed Miss Battle-Axe. 'Or playtime is cancelled. For everyone.'

Horrid Henry scowled. Why oh why did he have to come to school? Why didn't the Killer Boy Rats start a school, where you'd do nothing but scream and stomp all day? Now that's the sort of school everyone would want to go to. But no. He had to come here. When he was king all schools would just teach jousting and spying and Terminator Gladiator would be head.

Henry looked at the clock. How could it be only 9.42? It felt like he'd been sitting here for ages. What he'd give to be lounging right now on the comfy black chair, eating crisps and watching *Hog House* . . .

'Today we have a very exciting project,' said Miss Battle-Axe.

Henry groaned. Miss Battle-Axe's idea of an exciting project and his were never the same. An exciting project would be building a time machine, or a let's see who can give Henry the most chocolate competition, or counting how many times he could hit Miss Battle-Axe with a water balloon.

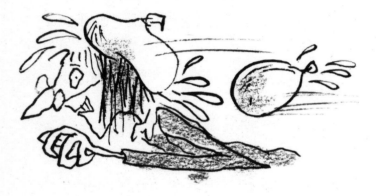

'We'll be writing autobiographies,' said Miss Battle-Axe.

Ha. He knew it would be something boring. Horrid Henry hated writing. All that pushing a pen across a piece of paper. Writing always made his hand ache. Writing was hard, heavy work. Why did Miss Battle-Axe try to torture him every day? Didn't she have anything better to do? Henry groaned again.

'An autobiography means the story of your life,' continued Miss Battle-Axe, glaring at him with her evil red eyes. 'Everyone will write a page about themselves and all the interesting things they've done.'

Yawn. Could his life get any worse?

Write a page? A whole entire page? What could be more boring then writing on and on about himself—

Wait a minute.

He got to write . . . about himself? The world's most fascinating boy? He could write for hours about himself! Days. Weeks. Years. Hold on . . . what was batty old Miss Battle-Axe saying now?

'. . . the really exciting part is that our autobiographies will be published in the local newspaper next week.'

Oh wow! Oh wow! Oh wow! His autobiography would be published!

This was his chance to tell the world all about being Lord High Excellent Majesty of the Purple Hand Gang. How he'd vanquished so many evil enemies. All the brilliant tricks he'd played on Peter. He'd write about the Mega-Mean Time Machine. And the Fangmangler. And the millions of times he'd defeated the Secret Club and squished Moody Margaret to a pulp! And oh yes, he'd be sure to include the time he'd turned his one line in the school play into a starring part and scored the winning goal in the class football match. But one page would barely cover one day in his life.

He needed hundreds of pages . . . no, thousands of pages to write about just some of his top triumphs.

Where to begin?

'Let's start with you, Clare,' burbled Miss Battle-Axe. 'What would you put in your autobiography?'

Clare beamed. 'I walked when I was four months old, learned to read when I was two, did long division when I was three, built my first telescope when I was four, composed a symphony—'

'Thank you, Clare, I'm sure everyone
will look forward to learning more
about you,' said Miss Battle-Axe.
'Steven. What will—'

'Can't we just get started?' shouted
Henry. 'I've got masses to write.'

'As I was saying, before I was so
RUDELY interrupted,' said Miss
Battle-Axe, glaring, 'Steven, what
will you be writing about in your
autobiography?'

'Being a caveman,' grunted Stone-Age
Steven. 'Uggg.'

'Fascinating,' said Miss Battle-Axe.
'Bert! What's interesting
about your life?'

'I dunno,' said Beefy
Bert.
'Right,
then,
everyone get

to work,' said Miss Battle-Axe, fixing
Horrid Henry with her basilisk stare.

Horrid Henry wrote until his hand
ached. But he'd barely got to the
time he tricked Margaret into eating
glop before Miss Battle-Axe ordered
everyone to stop.

'But I haven't finished!' shouted
Horrid Henry.

'Tough,' said Miss Battle-Axe. 'Now,
before we send these autobiographies to
the newspaper, I'd like a few of you to
read yours aloud to the class. William,
let's start with you.'

Weepy William
burst into tears. 'I
don't want to go
first,' he wailed,
dabbing his eyes
with some loo paper.

'Read,' said Miss Battle-Axe.

WILLIAM'S AUTOBIOGRAPHY

I was born. I cried. A few years later my brother Neil was born. I cried. In school Toby broke my pencil. Margaret picked me last. When we had to build the Parthenon Henry took all my paper and then when I got some more it was dirty. I had to play a blade of grass in the Nativity play. I cried. I lost every race on Sports Day. I cried. Then I got nits. On the school trip to the Ice Cream Factory I did a wee in my pants. I cried. Nothing else has ever happened to me.

'Who's next?' asked Miss Battle-Axe. Horrid Henry's hand shot up. Miss Battle-Axe looked as if a zombie had just walked across her grave. Horrid

Henry never put his hand up.

'Linda,' said Miss Battle-Axe.

Lazy Linda woke up and yawned.

LINDA'S AUTOBIOGRAPHY

I've had many nice beds in my life.
First was my Moses basket. Then
my cot. Then my little bed. Then
my great big sleigh bed. Then my
princess bed with the curtains
and the yellow headboard. I've
also had a lot of duvets. First my

duvet had ducks on it. Then I got a new soft one with big fluffy clouds. Oooh, I am sleepy just thinking about it . . .

'We have time to hear one more,' said Miss Battle-Axe, scanning the class. Horrid Henry thought his arm would detach itself from his shoulder if he shoved it any higher. 'Margaret,' said Miss Battle-Axe.

Henry scowled. It was so unfair. No one wanted to know about that moody old grouch.

Moody Margaret swaggered to the front and noisily cleared her throat.

MARGARET'S AUTOBIOGRAPHY

Greetings, world. I'm very sad when I think that many of you reading this will never get to meet someone as amazing as me. But at least you can read something I've written, and you newspaper people should save this piece of paper, because I, Margaret, have touched it with my very own hands, and it's sure to be valuable in the future when I'm famous.

Let me tell you a few things about marvellous me. First, I am the leader of the Secret Club, which is always victorious against the pathetic and puny Purple Hand Gang next door. One reason we always destroy them, apart from my brilliant plotting, is because the Purple Hand's so-called leader, Henry, is really stupid and useless and pathetic.

Horrid Henry could not believe his ears.

'Liar!' shouted Henry. 'I always win!'

'Shh!' said Miss Battle-Axe.

Naturally, I am the best footballer
the school has ever had or will ever have,
and naturally I'm Captain of the
Football Team. Everyone always
wants to play on my team, but of
course I don't let no-hopers like
Henry on it. I'm also a fantastic
trumpet player, and a top spy.
My best toy is my Dungeon
Drink Kit, which I've used many
times to play great tricks on the
Purple Hand Gang, which they
always fall for.

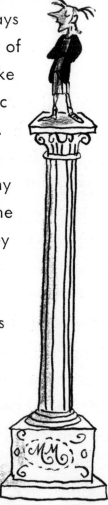

But I know I'll be very famous
so I'm saving my best stories
for my future best-selling
autobiography. I expect
there will be many statues
built to me all over
town, and that this

school will be renamed the
Margaret School.

I know it's hard realising that you can never
be as great as me, but get used to it!!!

Moody Margaret stopped reading
and swaggered to her seat.

'Yay!' yelled Sour Susan.

'Boo!' yelled Horrid Henry.

'Boo!' yelled Rude Ralph.

'There's no booing in this class,' said
Miss Battle-Axe.

Horrid Henry was outraged.
Margaret's lies about him . . . published?
The Purple Hand Gang always won.
But the whole world would believe
her lies once they read them in a
newspaper. He had to stop that foul
fiend. He had to show everyone what
a pants-face liar Margaret really was.

But how? How? He could just try to steal her autobiography. But someone might notice it had gone missing. Or he could . . . he could . . .

The playtime bell rang. Miss Battle-Axe starting collecting up all the autobiographies. Henry watched helplessly as Margaret's pack of boasting lies went into the folder.

And then Horrid Henry knew what he had to do. It was dangerous. It was risky. But a pirate gang leader had to take his chances, come what may.

Horrid Henry put up his hand. 'Please, miss, I haven't finished my autobiography yet. Could I stay in at playtime to finish?'

Miss Battle-Axe looked at Henry as if he had just grown an extra head. Henry . . . asking to spend more time on work? Horrid Henry asking to skip playtime?

'You can have five more minutes,' said Miss Battle-Axe, mopping her brow.

Horrid Henry wrote and wrote and wrote. When would Miss Battle-Axe leave him alone for a moment? But there she was, stapling up drawings of light bulbs.

'Put it in the folder with the others,' said Miss Battle-Axe, facing the wall. Horrid Henry didn't wait to be asked twice and grabbed the folder.

There wasn't a moment to lose. Henry rifled through the autobiographies, removed Margaret's, and substituted his new, improved version.

Moody Margaret peered round the door. Tee hee, thought Horrid Henry, pushing past her. Wouldn't she get a shock when she got her newspaper! What he'd give to see her face.

THWACK!

The local paper dropped through the door. Henry snatched it. There was the headline:

LOCAL CHILDREN SHINE IN FASCINATING TALES OF THEIR LIVES

Feverishly, he turned to read the class autobiographies.

MARGARET'S AUTOBIOGRAPHY

Oh woe is me, to be such a silly moody grouchy grump. I've always looked like a frog, in fact my mum took one look at me when I was born, threw me in the bin and ran screaming from the room. I don't blame her; I scream too whenever I see my ugly

warty face in the mirror. Everyone calls me Maggie Moo Moo, or Maggie Poo Poo, because I still wear nappies.

I started a Secret Club, which no

one wants to join, because I am so mean and bossy. I can't even have a sleepover without everyone running away. I keep trying to beat Henry's Purple Hand Gang, but he's much too clever for me and always foils my evil plans. I live next door to Henry, but of course I don't deserve such a

great honour. I really should just live in a smelly hole somewhere with all the other frogs. So, just remember, everyone, beware of being a moody, grouchy grump, or you might end up as horrible as me.

Yes! What a triumph! He was brilliant. He was a genius. What an amazing trick to write the truth about Margaret and swap it for her pack of lies.

Horrid Henry beamed. Now to enjoy his own autobiography. It was far too short, but there was always next time.

HENRY'S AUTOBIOGRAPHY

I'm a total copycat. Luckily, I live next door to the amazing Margaret, who I look up to and admire and worship more than anyone in the world. Margaret is my heroine, but I will

never be as clever or as brilliant as she
is, because I'm a pathetic, useless toad.
I copied her amazing Secret Club,
but the Purple Hand always loses. I
tried to do Makeovers, but of course I
couldn't. Even my own brother wants
to work for her as a spy. But then, she
is an empress and I'm a worm.

The most
exciting
thing
that ever
happened
to me was

when Margaret moved in next door.
I hope that one day she will let me
be the guard of the Secret Club, but I
will have to work very hard to deserve
it. That would be the best thing that
has ever happened in my boring life.

Huh? What? That fiend! That foul fiend!

The doorbell rang.

There was Margaret, waving the newspaper. Her face was purple.

'How dare you!' she shrieked.

'How dare you!' Henry shrieked.

'I'll get you for this, Henry,' hissed Margaret.

'Just you wait, Margaret,' hissed Henry.

4

HORRID HENRY ROCKS

'Boys, I have a very special treat for you,' said Mum, beaming.

Horrid Henry looked up from his *Mutant Max* comic.

Perfect Peter looked up from his spelling homework.

A treat? A special treat? A very special treat? Maybe Mum and Dad were finally appreciating him. Maybe they'd got tickets . . . maybe they'd actually got tickets . . . Horrid Henry's heart leapt. Could it be possible that at last, at long last, he'd get to go to a Killer Boy Rats concert?

'We're going to the Daffy and her Dancing Daisies show!' said Mum. 'I got the last four tickets.'

'OOOOOOHHHH,' said Peter, clapping his hands. 'Yippee! I love Daffy.'

What?? NOOOOOOOOOOOO! That wasn't a treat. That was torture. A treat would be a day at the Frosty Freeze Ice Cream Factory. A treat would be no school. A treat would be all he could eat at Gobble and Go.

'I don't want to see that stupid Daffy,' said Horrid Henry. 'I want to see the Killer Boy Rats.'

'No way,' said Mum.

'I don't like the Killer Boy Rats,' shuddered Peter. 'Too scary.'

'Me neither,' shuddered Mum. 'Too loud.'

'Me neither,' shuddered Dad. 'Too shouty.'

'NOOOOOOOO!' screamed Henry.

'But Henry,' said Peter, 'everyone loves Daffy.'

'Not me,' snarled Henry.

Perfect Peter waved a leaflet. 'Daffy's going to be the greatest show ever. Read this.'

Daffy sings and dances her way across the stage and into your heart. Your chance to sing-along to all your favourite daisy songs! I'm a Lazy Daisy. Whoops-a-Daisy. And of course, Upsy-Daisy, Crazy Daisy, Prance and Dance-a-Daisy.

✳

With special guest star Busy Lizzie!!!

AAAAARRRRRGGGGGHHHHHH.

Moody Margaret's parents were taking
her to the Killer Boy Rats concert.
Rude Ralph was going to the Killer
Boy Rats concert. Even Anxious
Andrew was going, and he didn't even
like them. Stuck-Up Steve had been
bragging for months that he was going
and would be sitting in a special box. It
was so unfair.

No one was a bigger Rats fan than
Horrid Henry. Henry
had all their albums:
Killer Boy Rats
Attack-Tack-Tack,
Killer Boy Rats Splat!

Killer
Boy Rats
Manic Panic.
'It's not fair!'
screamed Horrid
Henry. 'I want to see

the Killers!!!!'

'We have to see something that everyone in the family will like,' said Mum. 'Peter's too young for the Killer Boy Rats but we can all enjoy Daffy.'

'Not me!' screamed Henry.

Oh, why did he have such a stupid nappy baby for a brother? Younger brothers should be banned. They just wrecked everything. When he was King Henry the Horrible, all younger brothers would be arrested and dumped in a volcano.

In fact, why wait?

Horrid Henry pounced. He was a fiery god scooping up a human sacrifice and hurling him into the volcano's molten depths.

'AAAIIIIIEEEEEEE!' screamed
Perfect Peter. 'Henry attacked me.'

'Stop being horrid, Henry!' shouted
Mum. 'Leave your brother alone.'

'I won't go to Daffy,' yelled Henry.
'And you can't make me.'

'Go to your room,' said Dad.

Horrid Henry paced up and down his
bedroom, singing his favourite Rats
song at the top of his lungs:

92

I'M dead, you're dead, we're dead.
Get over it.
Dead is great, dead's where it's at
'Cause . . .

'Henry! Be quiet!' screamed Dad.

'I am being quiet!' bellowed Henry.
Honestly. Now, how could he get out
of going to that terrible Daffy concert?
He'd easily be the oldest one there.
Only stupid babies liked Daffy. If the
horrible songs didn't kill him then he
was sure to die of embarrassment. Then
they'd be sorry they'd made him go.
But it would be too late. Mum and Dad
and Peter could sob and boo hoo all
they liked but he'd still be dead. And
serve them right for being so mean to
him.

Dad said if he was good he could see
the Killer Boys next time they were
in town. Ha. The Killer Boy Rats

NEVER gave concerts. Next time they did he'd be old and hobbling and whacking Peter with his cane.

He had to get a Killer Boys ticket now. He just had to. But how? They'd been sold out for weeks.

Maybe he could place an ad:

Can you help?
Deserving Boy suffering from rare and terrible illness. His ears are falling off. Doctor has prescribed the Killer Boy Rats cure. Only by hearing the Rats live is there any hope. If you've got a ticket to the concert on Saturday PLEASE send it to Henry NOW.
(If you don't you know you'll be sorry.)

That might work. Or he could tell
people that the concert was cursed and
anyone who went would turn into a
rat. Hmmm. Somehow Henry didn't
see Margaret falling for that. Too bad
Peter didn't have a ticket, thought
Henry sadly, he could tell him he'd turn
into a killer and Peter would hand over
the ticket instantly.

And then suddenly Horrid Henry
had a brilliant, spectacular idea. There
must be someone out there who was
desperate for a Daffy ticket. In fact there
must be someone out there who would
swap a Killers ticket for a Daffy one. It
was certainly worth a try.

'Hey, Brian, I hear you've got a Killer
Boy Rats ticket,' said Horrid Henry at
school the next day.

'So?' said Brainy Brian.

'I've got a ticket to something much
better,' said Henry.

'What?' said Brian. 'The Killers are
the best.'

Horrid Henry could barely force
the grisly words out of his mouth. He
twisted his lips into a smile.

'Daffy and her Dancing Daisies,' said
Horrid Henry.

Brainy Brian stared at him.

'Daffy and her Dancing Daisies?' he
spluttered.

'Yes,' said Horrid Henry brightly.
'I've heard it's their best show ever.
Great new songs. You'd love it. Wanna
swap?'

Brainy Brian stared at him as if he had
a turnip instead of a head.

'You're trying to swap Daffy and her
Dancing Daisies tickets for the Killer
Boy Rats?' said Brian slowly.

'I'm doing you a favour, no one likes the Killer Boy Rats any more,' said Henry.

'I do,' said Brian.

Rats.

'How come you have a ticket for Daffy?' said Brian. 'Isn't that a baby show?'

'It's not mine, I found it,' said Horrid Henry quickly. Oops.

'Ha ha Henry, I'm seeing the Killers, and you're not,' Margaret taunted.

'Yeah Henry,' said Sour Susan.

'I heard . . .' Margaret doubled over laughing, 'I heard you were going to the Daffy show!'

'That's a big fat lie,' said Henry hotly. 'I wouldn't be seen dead there.'

Horrid Henry looked around the auditorium at the sea of little baby

nappy faces. There was Needy Neil
clutching his mother's hand. There
was Weepy William, crying because
he'd dropped his ice cream. There was
Toddler Tom, up past his bedtime.
Oh, no! There was Lisping Lily. Henry
ducked.

Phew. She hadn't seen him. Margaret
would never stop teasing him if she ever
found out. When he was king, Daffy
and her Dancing Daisies would live in
a dungeon with only rats for company.
Anyone who so much as mentioned
the name Daffy, or even grew a daisy,
would be flushed down the toilet.

There was a round of polite applause
as Daffy and her Dancing Daisies
pirouetted on stage. Horrid Henry
slumped in his seat as far as he could
slump and pulled his cap over his face.
Thank goodness he'd come disguised

and brought some earplugs. No one
would ever know he'd been.

'Tra la la la la la la!' trilled the Daisies.
'Tra la la la la la la!' trilled the
audience.

Oh, the torture, groaned Horrid
Henry as horrible song followed
horrible song. Perfect Peter sang along.
So did Mum and Dad.

AAARRRRRGGGHHHHH. And

to think that tomorrow night the Killer Boy Rats would be performing . . . and he wouldn't be there! It was so unfair.

Then Daffy cartwheeled to the front of the stage. One of the daisies stood beside her holding a giant hat.

'And now the moment all you Daffy Daisy fans have been waiting for,' squealed Daffy. 'It's the Lucky Ducky Daisy Draw, when we call up on stage an oh-so-lucky audience member to lead us in the Whoops-a-Daisy sing-a-long song! Who's it going to be?'

'Me!' squealed Peter. Mum squeezed his arm.

Daffy fumbled in the hat and pulled out a ticket.

'And the lucky winner of our ticket raffle is . . . Henry! Ticket 597! Ticket 597, yes Henry, you in row P, seat 10, come on up! Daffy needs you on stage!'

Horrid Henry was stuck to his seat in horror. It must be some other Henry. Never in his worst nightmares had he ever imagined—

'Henry, that's you,' said Perfect Peter. 'You're so lucky.'

'Henry! Come on up, Henry!' shrieked Daffy. 'Don't be shy!'

On stage at the Daffy show? No!

No! Wait till Moody Margaret found
out. Wait till anyone found out. Henry
would never hear the end of it. He
wasn't moving. Pigs would fly before he
budged.

'Henwy!' squealed Lisping Lily behind
him. 'Henwy! I want to give you a big
kiss, Henwy . . .'

Horrid Henry leapt out of his
seat. Lily! Lisping Lily! That fiend in
toddler's clothing would stop at nothing
to get hold of him.

Before Henry knew what had
happened, ushers dressed as daisies had
nabbed him and pushed him on stage.

Horrid Henry blinked in the lights.
Was anyone in the world as unlucky as
he?

'All together now, everyone get ready
to ruffle their petals. Let's sing Tippy-
toe daisy do / Let us sing a song for
you!' beamed Daffy. 'Henry, you start
us off.'

Horrid Henry stared at the vast
audience. Everyone was looking at him.
Of course he didn't know any stupid
Daisy songs. He always blocked his ears
or ran from the room whenever Peter
sang them. Whatever could the words
be . . . 'Watch out, whoop-di-do /
Daisy's doing a big poo?'

These poor stupid kids. If only they
could hear some decent songs, like . . .

like . . .

**'Granny on her crutches
Push her off her chair
Shove Shove Shove Shove
Shove her down the stairs.'**

shrieked Horrid Henry.

The audience was silent. Daffy looked stunned.

'Uh, Henry . . . that's not Tippy-toe daisy do,' whispered Daffy.

'C'mon everyone, join in with me,' shouted Horrid Henry, spinning round and twirling in his best Killer Boy Rats manner.

'I'm in my coffin
No time for coughin'
When you're squished down dead.
Don't care if you're a boffin
Don't care if you're a loony,
Don't care if you're cartoony
I'll squish you!'

sang Horrid Henry as loud as he could.

'Gonna be a rock star (and you ain't)
Don't even—'

Two security guards ran on stage and grabbed Horrid Henry.

'Killer Boy Rats forever!' shrieked Henry, as he was dragged off.

✳

Horrid Henry stared at the special delivery letter covered in skulls and crossbones. His hand shook.

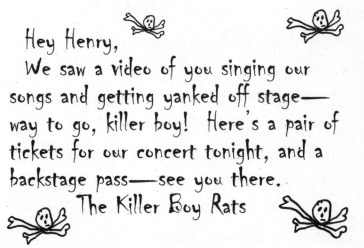

Hey Henry,
 We saw a video of you singing our songs and getting yanked off stage— way to go, killer boy! Here's a pair of tickets for our concert tonight, and a backstage pass—see you there.
            The Killer Boy Rats

Horrid Henry goggled at the tickets
and the backstage pass. He couldn't
move. He couldn't breathe. He was
going to the Killer Boy Rats concert.
He was actually going to the Killer Boy
Rats concert.

Life, thought Horrid Henry, beaming,
was sweet.

ACKNOWLEDGEMENTS

Thanks to Hannah Goodwin, who suggested Horrid Henry's Autobiography would be a good title for a story. And thanks to Michael Rosen for the muddy twig revenge, and to my son Josh, who came up with an extraordinary number of excellent tricks for Henry to play on Peter.

HORRID HENRY
and the
Zombie Vampire

For the amazing, inspiring, and fantastic
Josh Stamp-Simon

CONTENTS

1

HORRiD HENRY WRITES A STORY

'NO!' screamed Horrid Henry. 'NO!'

'Don't be horrid, Henry,' said Dad.

'We'd LOVE to hear your new story, Peter,' said Mum.

'I wouldn't,' said Henry.

'Don't be rude, Henry,' said Dad.

Horrid Henry stuck his fingers in his ears and glared.

AAAARRRRRGGGGHHHHH.

Wasn't it bad enough that he had to sit at the table in front of a disgusting plate filled with – yuck – sprouts and – bleccchh – peas instead of the chips

and pizza he had BEGGED Dad to
cook for dinner? Did he really have to
listen to Peter droning on as well?

This was torture. This was a cruel and
unusual punishment. Did any child in
the world ever suffer as much as Henry?

It was so unfair! Mum and Dad wouldn't
let him play the Killer Boy Rats during
dinner but now they wanted to force him
to listen to Peter read his stupid story.

Peter wrote the world's worst stories.
If they weren't about fairies, they were
about kittens, or butterflies, or little elves
that helped humans with their chores.
His last one was all about the stupid
adventures of Peter's favourite plastic
sheep, Fluff Puff, and the terrible day his

 pink and yellow nose turned
blue. The king of the sheep had
to come and wave his magic
hoof to change it back . . .

Henry shuddered just remembering.
And then Henry had shouted that a
woodsman who really fancied a lamb
chop had nabbed Fluff Puff and then
Mum and Dad had sent him to his room.

Perfect Peter unfolded his piece of
paper and cleared his throat.

'My story is called, *Butterfly Fairies
Paint the Rainbow*,' said Peter.

'AARRGGHHH!' said Henry.

'What a lovely title,' said Mum.
She glared at Henry.

'Can't wait to hear it,' said Dad.
'Stop playing with your food, Henry,'
he added, as Horrid Henry started
squishing peas under his knife.

'Once upon a time there lived seven
butterfly fairies. There was one for
every colour of the rainbow. Dance
and prance, prance and dance, went the
butterfly fairies every day.'

Henry groaned. 'That's just copying
Daffy and her Dancing Daisies.'

'I'm not copying,' said Perfect Peter.

'Are too.'

'Am not.'

'Don't be horrid, Henry,' said Mum.
'Peter, that's a lovely story so far. Go
on, what happens next?'

'The butterfly fairies also kept the
rainbow lovely and shiny. Each fairy
polished their own colour every day.
But one day the butterfly fairies looked

up at the sky. Whoopsydaisy! All the colours had fallen off the rainbow.'

'Call the police,' said Horrid Henry.

'Mum, Henry keeps interrupting me,' wailed Peter.

'Stop it, Henry,' said Mum.

'The fairies ran to tell their queen what had happened,' read Peter.

'"All the colours of the rainbow fell down," cried the butterfly fairies.

"Oh no."

"Oh woe."

"Boo hoo. Boo hoo.'"

SCRATCH! SCRAPE!

Horrid Henry started grinding his knife into his plate.

'Stop that, Henry,' said Dad.

'I'm just eating my dinner,' said Henry. He sighed loudly. 'You're always telling me to use my knife. And now I am and you tell me to stop.'

Perfect Peter raised his voice. '"Don't cry, butterfly fairies," said the Queen. "We'll just—"'

SCRAPE!

Horrid Henry scraped louder.

'Mum!' wailed Peter. 'He's trying to ruin my story.'

'There's nothing to ruin,' said Henry.

'Be quiet, Henry,' said Dad. 'I don't want to hear another word out of you.'

Henry burped.

'Henry! I'm warning you!'

'I didn't *say* anything,' said Henry.

'Mum! I'm just getting to the really exciting bit,' said Peter. 'Henry's spoiling it.'

'Go on Peter, we're all listening,' said Mum.

'"Don't cry, butterflies," said the Queen. "We'll just have to pick up our magic paint pots and colour it back in."

"Yay," said the fairies. "Let's get to work."'

'Blecchhhhhhh!' said Horrid Henry, pretending to vomit and knocking a few sprouts onto the floor.

'Henry, I'm warning you . . . ' said Mum. 'Sorry, Peter.'

'"I'll paint the rainbow blue," said blue butterfly.

"I'll paint the rainbow orange," said

orange butterfly.

"I'll paint the rainbow green," said green butterfly.

"I'll paint—"'

"'I'll paint the rainbow black and hang skulls on it," said Terminator butterfly,' snarled Horrid Henry.

'MUM!' wailed Peter. 'Henry's interrupting me *again*!'

'Henry, this is your final warning,' said Dad. 'If I hear one more word out of you, no TV for a week.'

'Then the Fairy Queen picked up the paint pots and—'

Horrid Henry yawned loudly.

' . . . and the butterfly fairies were so
happy that they began to sing:
  "Tee hee. Tra la.
  Tra la tra la
  We are dainty little fairies
  And we play and sing all day
  Maybe you can come and join us
  Then we'll paint the day away
  Tee hee hee hee
  Tra la la la."'

'Blah blah, blah blah,' snarled Horrid
Henry. He hadn't thought Peter could
write a worse story than *The Adventures
of Fluff Puff* but he was wrong.

'That's the worst story I ever heard,'
said Horrid Henry.

'Henry. Be quiet,' said Dad.

Horrid Henry's fingers curled around
a sprout.

'What did *you* think of my story,
Mum?' said Peter.

'That was the best story I ever heard,' said Mum.

'Well done Peter,' said Dad.

Bong! A sprout hit Perfect Peter on the head.

'OW! Henry just threw a sprout at me,' wailed Peter.

'Didn't!' said Henry. 'It slipped off my fork.'

'That's it, Henry!' shouted Dad.

'Go to your room, Henry!' shouted Mum.

Horrid Henry leapt down from the table and began to stomp. 'Look at me, I'm a butterfly fairy!'

Horrid Henry stomped upstairs to his bedroom. It was so unfair. In the olden days, when people hadn't enjoyed a play, didn't they throw tomatoes and rotten oranges at the stage? He was only being historical.

Peter was lucky he
hadn't thrown much
worse at him.
Well, he'd
show everyone
how it was
done.
He'd
write the
greatest
story ever.

All about King Hairy the Horrible
and his wicked
wife Queen
Gertrude the
Gruesome.
They would
spend their
days cackling
and making evil plans.

Horrid Henry lay down on his bed.

He'd get writing as soon as he finished this week's *Screamin' Demon* comic.

'Margaret! Stop shouting!
Steven! Stop grunting!
William! Stop weeping!
Soraya! Stop singing!
Henry! Just stop!
Everyone. BE QUIET!' yelled Miss Battle-Axe. She mopped her brow. One day she would retire to a war zone and enjoy the peace and quiet.

Until then . . . she glared at her class.

'Now. I want everyone to settle down and write a story.'

Horrid Henry scowled. Miss Battle-Axe always hated his stories, even Henry's brilliant one about the Troll Werewolf Mummies who hid beneath teachers' beds and snacked on their toes. She hadn't even liked his cannibal can-can story about the cannibal dance troupe who ate their way across Europe.

It was hard, heavy work writing a story. Why should he bother when his efforts met with so little reward?

What was that stupid thing Peter had read out last night? That would do. Quickly Horrid Henry scribbled down Peter's dreadful Butterfly Fairies story. Miss

Battle-Axe didn't deserve anything better.

Done! Now back to his comic. Screamin' Demon was just about to discover where the Master of the Macabre had hidden the treasure . . .

Horrid Henry felt a long fingernail poke into his shoulder. He looked up into Miss Battle-Axe's evil eye.

' . . . and why aren't you writing your story, Henry?' hissed Miss Battle-Axe.

Horrid Henry smiled.

'Because I've finished it,' said Henry.

'You . . . finished it?' said Miss Battle-Axe. She tugged on her ear. Perhaps it was time she had her earwax removed again.

'Yup,' said Henry.

'Let me see,' said Miss Battle-Axe, holding out her bony claw.

Tee hee, thought Horrid Henry, handing her the story. She doesn't

believe me. Wouldn't batty old Miss
Battle-Axe get a surprise.

'Hmmm,' said Miss Battle-Axe
after she'd finished reading. 'Hmmm.
Butterfly Fairies Paint the Rainbow.
Hmmm.' She stared at Henry and tried
to smile but her mouth had trouble
turning up due to lack of practice.
'*Much* better than usual, Henry.'

Henry stared. The men in white coats
would be coming to take Miss Battle-
Axe away any moment if she liked this
story better than his others.

'In fact . . . in fact . . . I want you to
go now to Miss Lovely's class and read it
out loud to the Infants. They'll love it.'

What? NO!!!!!!!

Perfect Peter's class sat expectantly on
the carpet as Horrid Henry stood before
them, story in hand. Now everyone

would think *he'd* written this stupid story. Moody Margaret would tease him until he was old and grey and toothless. But what could he do? He was trapped.

'*Putter fair pat the rainb . . .*' mumbled Horrid Henry.

'Speak up, Henry,' said Miss Lovely. 'Don't be shy. We're *so* looking forward to your story.'

'*Butterfly Fairies Paint the Rainbow,*' hissed Horrid Henry.

Perfect Peter's jaw dropped. Too late Henry realised his mistake. Writing a story about butterfly fairies was bad enough. But he'd never hear the end of it if people found out he'd *copied* his younger brother's story. Though even Peter wouldn't be such a tell-tale . . . would he?

Peter put his hand in the air.

'Miss Lovely, that's *my*—' began Peter.

'Just kidding,' said Horrid Henry
hastily. 'My story is really called, uh,
Butterfly Fairies Fight the Giants.'

He glanced down at his story,
changing words as he read:

'Once upon a time there lived two
hideous giants, King Hairy the Horrible
and Queen Gertrude the Gruesome.
Stamp and stomp, stomp and stamp
went the hideous giants every day.

They liked stomping on fairies,

especially the butterfly fairies who polished the rainbow every day.

One day the giants looked up at the sky. Whoopsydaisy! All the butterfly fairies had fallen off the rainbow.

"Oh what fun," cackled King Hairy the Horrible, squishing the blue butterfly fairy.

"Yippee!" squealed Queen Gertrude the Gruesome, squashing the orange butterfly fairy.

"Ha ha!" they both shrieked, stomping on the green butterfly fairy.'

Perky Parveen looked shocked.

Spotless Sam began to sniff.

"'I'm going to roast those fairies for dinner," said Queen Gertrude the Gruesome. "Yum, yum!" she drooled, as the delicious smell of cooked fairy wafted through the castle kitchen. Then the Queen picked up the fairy bones and—'

132

Miss Lovely looked pale.

Oh no, what now, thought Horrid Henry desperately. He'd reached Peter's horrible fairy song.

"Tee hee. Tra la.

Tra la tra la

We are dainty little fairies

And we play and sing all day

Maybe you can come and join us

Then we'll paint the day away

Tee hee hee hee

Tra la la la."

Horrid Henry took a deep breath.

133

'King Hairy the Horrible and Queen Gertrude the Gruesome were so happy that they began to sing:
"Tee hee. Ha ha. Ha ha ha ha.
We are big and ugly giants
And we belch and kill all day
Maybe we can come and find you
Then we'll squish your guts away
Tee hee tee hee
Ha ha ha ha,"
bellowed Horrid Henry.

Perky Parveen began to cry.

'The fairwies got squished,' sobbed Lisping Lily.

'I don't want the giants to eat the fairies,' shrieked Tidy Ted.

'I'm scared,' howled Helpful Hari.

'I want my Mama,' wept Needy Neil.

'Wah!' wailed the Infants.

Horrid Henry was thrilled. What a reaction! Maybe I'll add a bit more,

thought Horrid Henry. This is such a great story it's a shame to end it here.

'Let's find some bunnies,' snarled the giants. 'I'm sure—'

'Stop! Stop!' said Miss Lovely. She looked ashen. 'Better go back to your class,' she whispered. What had Miss Battle-Axe been thinking?

Horrid Henry shook his head and closed the door on the screaming, howling class.

Wow. What a great story he'd written.

Maybe he should be an author when he grew up.

....

HORRiD HENRY AND THE NUDIE FOODIE

'Children, I have some *thrilling* news,' burbled Mrs Oddbod.

Horrid Henry groaned. His idea of thrilling news and Mrs Oddbod's idea of thrilling news were not the same. Thrilling news would be Mutant Max replacing Mrs Oddbod as head. Thrilling news would be Miss Battle-Axe being whisked off to ancient Rome to be a gladiator. Thrilling news would be Moody Margaret dumped in a swamp and Perfect Peter sent to prison.

Thrilling news wasn't new coat hooks and who was in the Good as Gold book.

But wait. What was Mrs Oddbod saying? 'Our school has been chosen to be a healthy-eating school. Our new healthy and nutritious school meals will be an example for schools everywhere.'

Horrid Henry sat up. What? *Healthy* eating? Oh no.

Henry knew what grown-ups meant by healthy food. Celery. Beetroot. Aubergine towers. Anything that tasted yucky and looked

revolting was bound
to be good for him.
Anything that tasted
yummy was bound
to be bad. Henry had plenty of healthy
eating at home. Was
nowhere safe?

'And guess
who's going to
help make our

school a beacon of
healthy eating?' babbled
Mrs Oddbod. 'Only
the world-famous chef,
Mr Nudie Foodie.'

Rude Ralph snorted. 'Nudie,'
he jeered.

Mr Nudie Foodie? thought
Horrid Henry. What kind of
stupid name was that? Were
there really parents out there

whose surname was Foodie, who'd
decided that the perfect name for their
son was Nudie?

'And here he is, in person,'
proclaimed Mrs Oddbod.

The children clapped as a shaggy-
haired man wearing a red-checked
apron and a chef's hat bounced to the
front of the auditorium.

'From today your school will be *the* place for delicious, nutritious food,' he beamed. 'I'm not nude, it's my food that's nude! My delicious, yummalicious grub is just plain scrummy.'

Horrid Henry couldn't believe his ears. Just plain, delicious food? Why, that was *exactly* what Horrid Henry loved. Plain burgers. Plain pizzas just with cheese and nothing else. No sneaky flabby pieces of aubergine or grisly chunks of red pepper ruining the topping. Plain chips slathered in ketchup. No funny bits. No strange green stuff. Three cheers to more burgers, more chips and more pizza!

Horrid Henry could see it now. Obviously, *he'd* be asked to create the yummy new school menu of plain, delicious food.

Monday: crisps, chips, ice cream, cake, burgers

Tuesday: burgers, chips, crisps, chocolate

Wednesday: pizza, chips, crisps, ice cream

Thursday: chocolate cake

Friday: burgers, pizza, chips, crisps, cake, ice cream

(after all, it was the end of the week, and nice to celebrate). Oh, and fizzywizz drinks every day, and chocolate milk. There! A lovely, healthy, plain, nutritious and delicious menu that everyone would love. Because, let's face it, at the moment school dinners *were* horrid. They only served burgers and chips once a week,

thought Horrid Henry indignantly.
Well, he'd soon sort *that* out.

In fact, maybe *he* should be a famous
chef when he got older. Chef Henry,
the burger wizard. Happy Henry,
hamburger hero. He would open a
chain of famous restaurants, called
Henry's! Where the eatin' can't be
beaten! Hmmm, well, he'd have
time to improve the name, while
collecting his millions every week
from the restaurant tills
as happy customers
fought their way
inside for the chance
to chow down
on one of Happy
Henry's bun-tastic
burgers. Kids
everywhere
would beg to

143

eat there, safe in the knowledge that no vegetables would ever contaminate their food. Ahhh! Horrid Henry sighed.

Mr Nudie Foodie was leaping up and down with excitement. 'And you're all going to help me make the delicious food that will be a joy to eat. Remember, just like the words to my hit song:

It's not rude
To be a dude

Who loves nude food.
Yee haw.'

'Well, Nudie,' said Mrs Oddbod. 'Uhh, I mean, Mr Foodie . . . '

'Just call me Mr Nudie Foodie,' said Mr Nudie Foodie. 'Now, who wants to be a nudie foodie and join me in the kitchen to make lunch today?'

'Me!' shouted Perfect Peter.

'Me!' shouted Clever Clare.

'I want to be a nudie foodie,' said Jolly Josh.

'I want to be a nudie foodie,' said Tidy Ted.

'I want to be a nudie foodie,' yelled Greedy Graham. 'I think.'

'A healthy school is a happy school,' said Mr Nudie Foodie, beaming. 'My motto is: Only bad food boos, when you choose yummy food. And at lunchtime today, all your parents will be coming to the cafeteria to sample our scrumptious, yummalicious, fabulicious and irresistible new food! Olé!'

Horrid Henry looked round the school kitchen. He'd never seen so many pots and pans and vats and cauldrons. So this was where the school glop was made.

Well, not any longer. Would they be making giant whopper burgers in the huge frying pans? Or vats and vats of chips in the huge pots? Maybe they'd make pizzas for the gigantic ovens!

The Nudie Foodie stood before Henry's class. 'This is so exciting,' he said bouncing up and down. 'Everyone ready to make some delicious food?'

'Yes!' bellowed Henry's class.

'Right, then, let's get cooking,' said Mr Nudie Foodie.

Horrid Henry stood in front of a chopping board with Weepy William, Dizzy Dave and Fiery Fiona. Fiery Fiona shoved Henry.

'Stop hogging the chopping board,' she hissed.

 Horrid Henry shoved her back, knocking the

lumpy bag of ingredients onto the floor.

'Stop hogging it yourself,' he hissed back.

'Wah!' wailed Weepy William.

 'Henry pushed me.'
Wait. What was rolling all over the floor? It looked like . . . it couldn't be . . .

'Group 1, here's how to slice a yummy green pepper,' beamed Mr Nudie Foodie. 'And Group 2, you're in charge of the tomatoes . . . Group 3, you make the broccoli salad. Group 4 will look after the mushrooms.'

 Green pepper? Tomatoes? Broccoli? Mushrooms? What was this muck?

'It's my yummy, scrummy, super, secret, vege-tastic pasta sauce!' said Mr Nudie Foodie.

What? What a dirty rotten trick. Where were the chips? Where were the burgers?

And then suddenly Horrid Henry understood Mr Nudie Foodie's evil plan. He was going to sneak *vegetables* onto the school menu. Not just a single vegetable, but loads and loads and loads of vegetables. Enough evil vegetables to kill someone a hundred times over. Boy impaled by killer carrot.

Girl chokes
to death
on deadly
broccoli.
Boy gags on
toxic tomato.
Henry could see
the headlines now.
They'd find him dead in the
lunchroom, poisoned
by vegetables, his
limbs twisted in
agony . . .

Well, *no way*.
No way was
this foul fiend
going to trick
Henry into eating
vegetables.

Everyone chopped and stirred and
mixed. The evil brew hissed and

bubbled. Horrid Henry had never felt
so cheated in his life.

Finally, the bell rang.

Mr Nudie Foodie stood by the exit
with an enormous black bin bag.

'Before you leave I want you to open
your lunch boxes and dump all your
junk food in here. No need for that
stuff today.'

'Huh?' said Rude Ralph.

'No!' wailed Greedy Graham.

'Yes!' said Mr Nudie Foodie. 'You'll thank me later.'

Horrid Henry gasped in horror as everyone threw their yummy snacks into the bag as they filed out of the kitchen and ran out for playtime. For once Henry was glad his mean, horrible parents never packed anything good in *his* lunchbox.

Was there no end to this evil man's plots? thought Horrid Henry, stomping past Mr Nudie Foodie into the hall. First, vegetable pasta sauce, then stealing everyone's sweets? What a waste. All those treats going straight into the bin . . .

'Rescue us Henry!' squealed the chocolate and crisps trapped inside the bin bag. 'Help!'

Horrid Henry didn't need to be asked twice. He crept down the hall and darted back into the school kitchen.

Sweets, here I come, thought Horrid Henry.

The kitchen was empty. Huge vats of vegetable sauce sat ready to be poured onto pasta. What horrors would Mr Nudie Foodie try to sneak on the menu tomorrow? And the next day? And the next? Just wait until the parents discovered the sauce was made of vegetables. They'd make the children eat this swill every day.

AAAAARRRRRGGGHHHHH.

And then suddenly Horrid Henry knew what he had to do. He looked longingly at the enormous black bin bag bulging with crisps and chocolate

and yummy snacks. Horrid Henry gritted his teeth. Sometimes you had to think ahead. Sometimes you couldn't be distracted. Not even by doughnuts.

There wasn't a moment to lose. Any second a teacher or dinner lady could come in and foil him. He had to seize

his chance to stop Mr Nudie Foodie
once and for all.

Grabbing whatever was nearest,
Horrid Henry emptied a tin of salt into
the first vat of sauce. Into the second
went a tin of mustard powder. Into the
third went a bottle of vinegar. Into the
fourth and final one . . .

Henry looked at the gurgling, bubbling,
poisonous, reeking, rancid, toxic sauce.
Take that, Nudie Foodie, thought Horrid

Henry, reaching for a tub of lard.

'What are you doing, Henry?' rasped a deadly voice.

Henry froze.

'Just looking for my lunchbox,' he said, pretending to search behind the cooking pots.

Miss Battle-Axe snarled, flashing her yellow brick teeth. She pointed to the door. Horrid Henry ran out.

Phew. What a lucky escape. Shame he hadn't completed his mission, but three vats out of four wasn't bad. Anyway, the fourth pot was sure to be disgusting, even without extra dollops of lard.

You are dead meat, Mr Nudie Foodie, thought Horrid Henry.

'Parents, children, prepare yourselves for a taste sensation!' said Mr Nudie Foodie, ladling out pasta and sauce.

Lazy Linda's mother took a big forkful. 'Hmm, doesn't this look yummy!' she said. 'It's about time this school served proper food,' said Moody Margaret's mum, shovelling an enormous spoonful into her mouth.

'I couldn't agree more,' said Tidy Ted's dad, scooping up pasta.

'BLECCCCHHHHH!' spluttered Margaret's mother, spitting it out all over Aerobic Al's Dad. Her face was

purple. 'That's disgusting! My Maggie Moo-Moo won't be touching a drop of that!'

'What are you trying to do, poison people?!' screamed Aerobic Al's Dad. His face was green.

'I'm not eating this muck!' shouted Clever Clare's Mum. 'And Clare certainly isn't.'

'But . . . but . . . ' gasped Mr Nudie Foodie. 'This sauce is my speciality, it's delicious, it's—' he took a mouthful.

'Uggghhhh,' he said, spewing it all over Mrs Oddbod. 'It *is* disgusting.'

Wow, thought Horrid Henry. Wow. Could the sauce really be *so* bad? He had to try it. Would he get the salty, the mustardy, the vinegary, or just the plain disgusting vegetably?

Henry picked up a tiny forkful of pasta, put it in his mouth and swallowed.

He was still breathing. He was still alive. Everyone at his table was slurping up the food and beaming. Everyone at the other tables was coughing and choking and spitting . . .

Horrid Henry took another teeny tiny taste.

The sauce was . . . delicious. It was much nicer than the regular glop they served at lunchtime with pasta. It was a million billion times nicer. And he had just . . . he had just . . .

'Is this some kind of joke?' gasped Mrs Oddbod, gagging. 'Mr Nudie Foodie,

you are toast! Leave here at once!'

Mr Nudie Foodie slunk off.

'NOOOOO!' screamed Horrid
Henry. 'It's yummy! Don't go!'

Everyone stared at Horrid Henry.

'Weird,' said Rude Ralph.

3

HORRID HENRY AND THE MAD PROFESSOR

Horrid Henry grabbed the top secret sweet tin he kept hidden under his bed. It was jampacked with all his favourites: Big Boppers. Nose Pickers. Dirt Balls. Hot Snot. Gooey Chewies. Scrunchy Munchies.

Yummy!!!

Hmmm boy! Horrid Henry's mouth watered as he prised off the lid. Which to have first? A Dirt Ball? Or a Gooey Chewy? Actually, he'd just scoff the lot. It had been ages since he'd . . .

Huh?

Where were all his chocolates? Where were all his sweets? Who'd nicked them? Had Margaret invaded his room? Had Peter sneaked in? How dare—Oh. Horrid Henry suddenly remembered. *He'd* eaten them all.

Rats.

Rats.

Triple rats.

Well, he'd just have to go and buy more. He was sure to have loads of pocket money left.

Chocolate, here I come, thought Horrid Henry, heaving his bones and dashing over to his skeleton bank.

He shook it. Then he shook it again.

There wasn't even a rattle.

How could he have *no* money and *no* sweets? It was so unfair! Just last night Peter had been boasting about having £7.48 pence in *his* piggy bank. And loads of sweets left over from Hallowe'en. Horrid Henry scowled. Why did Peter *always* have money? Why did he, Henry, *never* have money?

Money was totally wasted on Peter. What was the point of Peter having pocket money since he never spent it? Come to think of it, what was the point of Peter having sweets since he never ate them?

There was a shuffling, scuttling noise, then Perfect Peter dribbled into Henry's bedroom carrying all his soft toys.

'Get out of my room, worm!' bellowed Horrid Henry, holding his nose. 'You're stinking it up.'

'I am not,' said Peter.

'Are too, smelly pants.'

'I do not have smelly pants,' said
Peter.

'Do too, woofy, poofy, pongy pants.'

Peter opened his mouth, then closed it.

'Henry, will you play with me?' said
Peter.

'No.'

'Please?'

'No!'

'Pretty please?'

'No!!'

'But we could play school with all my cuddly toys,' said Peter. 'Or have a tea party with them . . . '

'For the last time, NOOOOOOO!' screamed Horrid Henry.

'You *never* play with me,' said Perfect Peter.

'That's 'cause you're a toad-faced nappy wibble bibble,' said Horrid Henry. 'Now go away and leave me alone.'

'Mum! Henry's calling me names again!' screamed Peter. 'He called me wibble bibble.'

'Henry! Don't be horrid!' shouted Mum.

'I'm not being horrid, Peter's annoying me!' yelled Henry.

'Henry's annoying *me*!' yelled Peter.

'Make him stop!' screamed Henry and Peter.

Mum ran into the room.

'Boys. If you can't play nicely then leave each other alone,' said Mum.

'Henry won't play with me,' wailed Peter. 'He *never* plays with me.'

'Henry! Why can't you play with your brother?' said Mum. 'When I was little Ruby and I played beautifully together all the time.'

Horrid Henry scowled.

'Because he's a wormy worm,' said Henry.

'Mum! Henry just called me a wormy worm,' wailed Peter.

'Don't call your brother names,' said Mum.

'Peter only wants to play stupid baby games,' said Henry.

'I do not,' said Peter.

'If you're not going to play together then you can do your chores,' said Mum.

'I've done mine,' said Peter. 'I fed Fluffy, cleaned out the litter tray *and* tidied my room.'

Mum beamed. 'Peter, *you* are the best boy in the world.'

Horrid Henry scowled. He'd been far too busy reading his comics to empty the wastepaper bins and tidy his room.

He stuck out his tongue at Peter behind Mum's back.

'Henry's making horrible faces at me,' said Peter.

'Henry, *please* be nice for once and play with Peter,' said Mum. She sighed and left the room.

Henry glared at Peter.

Peter glared at Henry.

Horrid Henry was about to push Peter out the door when suddenly he had a brilliant, spectacular idea. It was so brilliant and so spectacular that Horrid Henry couldn't believe he was still standing in his bedroom and hadn't blasted off into outer space trailing clouds of glory. Why had he never thought of this before? It was magnificent. It was genius. One day he would start Henry's Genius Shop, where people would pay a million

pounds to buy his super fantastic ideas.
But until then . . .

'Okay Peter, I'll play with you,' said
Horrid Henry. He smiled sweetly.

Perfect Peter could hardly believe his
ears.

'You'll . . . *play* with me?' said Perfect
Peter.

'Sure,' said Horrid Henry.

'What do you want to play?' asked
Peter cautiously. The last time Peter
could remember Henry playing with
him they'd played Cannibals and
Dinner. Peter had had to be dinner . . .

'Let's play Robot and Mad Professor,'
said Henry.

'Okay,' said Perfect Peter. Wow. That
sounded a lot more exciting than his
usual favourite game – writing lists of

vegetables or having ladybird tea parties
with his stuffed toys. He'd probably
have to be the robot, and do what
Henry said, but it would be worth it,
to play such a fun game.

'I'll be the robot,' said Horrid Henry.

Peter's jaw dropped.

'Go on,' said Henry. 'You're the mad
professor. Tell me what to do.'

Wow. Henry was even letting *him* be
the mad professor! Maybe he'd been
wrong about Henry . . .
maybe Henry had been
struck by lightning
and changed into a
nice brother . . .

'Robot,' ordered
Perfect Peter. 'March around the room.'

Horrid Henry didn't budge.

'Robot!' said Peter. 'I order you to
march.'

'Pro—fes—sor! I— need—twenty- five p—to— move,' said Henry in a robotic voice. 'Twenty-five p. Twenty- p. Twenty-five p. Twenty-five p.'

'Twenty-five p?' said Peter.

'That's the rules of Robot and Mad Professor,' said Henry, shrugging.

'Okay Henry,' said Peter, rummaging in his bank. He handed Henry twenty-five p.

Yes! thought Horrid Henry.

Horrid Henry took a few stiff steps, then slowed down and stopped.

'More,' said robotic Henry. 'More. My batteries have run down. More.'

Perfect Peter handed over another

twenty-five p.

Henry lurched around for a few
more steps, crashed into the wall and
collapsed on the floor.

'I need sweets to get up,' said the
robot. 'Fetch me sweets. Systems
overload. Sweets. Sweets. Sweets.'

Perfect Peter dropped two sweets into
Henry's hand. Henry twitched his foot.

'More,' said the robot. 'Lots more.'

Perfect Peter dropped four more

sweets. Henry jerked up into a sitting position.

'I will now tell you my top secret—secret—secret—secret—' stuttered Horrid Henry. 'Cross—my—palm—with—silver and sweets . . . ' He held out his robot hands. Peter filled them.

Tee hee.

'I want to be the robot now,' said Peter.

'Okay, robot,' said Henry. 'Run upstairs and empty all the waste-paper baskets. Bet you can't do it in thirty seconds.'

'Yes I can,' said Peter.

'Nah, you're too rusty and puny,' said Horrid Henry.

'Am not,' said Peter.

'Then prove it, robot,' said Henry.

'But aren't you going to give me—' faltered Peter.

'MOVE!' bellowed Henry. 'They don't call me the MAD professor for nothing!!!'

Playing Robot and Mad Professor was a bit less fun than Peter had anticipated. Somehow, his piggy bank was now empty and Henry's skeleton bank was full. And somehow most of Peter's Hallowe'en sweets were now in Henry's sweet box.

Robot and Mad Professor was the most fun Henry had ever had playing with Peter. Now that he had all Peter's money and all Peter's sweets, could he trick Peter into doing all his chores as well?

'Let's play school,' said Peter. That would be safe. There was no way Henry could trick him playing *that* . . .

'I've got a better idea,' said Henry. 'Let's play Slaves and Masters. You're

175

the slave. I order you to . . . '

'No,' interrupted Peter. 'I don't want
to.' Henry couldn't make him.

'Okay,' said Henry. 'We can play
school. You can be the tidy monitor.'

Oh! Peter loved being tidy monitor.

'We're going to play Clean Up The
Classroom!' said Henry. 'The classroom
is in here. So, get to work.'

Peter looked around the great mess
of toys and dirty clothes and comics

and empty wrappers scattered all over Henry's room.

'I thought we'd start by taking the register,' said Peter.

'Nah,' said Henry. 'That's the baby way to play school. You have to start by tidying the classroom. You're the tidy monitor.'

'What are you?' said Peter.

'The teacher, of course,' said Henry.

'Can I be the teacher next?' said Peter.

'Sure,' said Henry. 'We'll swap after you finish your job.'

Henry lay on his bed and read his comic and stuffed the rest of Peter's sweets into his mouth. Peter tidied.

Ah, this was the life.

'It's very quiet in here,' said Mum, popping her head round the door. 'What's going on?'

'Nothing,' said Horrid Henry.

'Why is Peter tidying your room?' said Mum.

''Cause he's the tidy monitor,' said Henry.

Perfect Peter burst into tears. 'Henry's taken all my money and all my sweets and made me do all his chores,' he wailed.

'Henry!' shouted Mum. 'You horrid boy!'

★

On the bad side, Mum made Henry give Peter back all his money. But on the good side, all his chores were done for the week. And he couldn't give Peter back his sweets because he'd eaten them all.

Result!

4

HORRID HENRY AND THE ZOMBIE VAMPIRE

'Isn't it exciting, Henry?' said Perfect Peter, packing Bunnykins carefully in his Sammy the Snail overnight bag. 'A museum sleepover! With a torch-lit trail! And worksheets! I can't think of anything more fun.'

'I can,' snarled Horrid Henry. Being trapped in a cave with Clever Clare reciting all the multiplication tables from one to a million. Watching *Cooking Cuties*. Even visiting Nurse Needle for one of her horrible injections. (Well, maybe not *that*).

But *almost* anything would be better than being stuck overnight in Our Town Museum on a class sleepover. No TV. No computers. No comics. Why oh why did he have to do this? He wanted to sleep in his own comfy bed, not in a sleeping bag on the museum's cold hard floor, surrounded by photos of old mayors and a few dusty exhibits.

AAARRRRGGGHH. Wasn't it bad enough he was bored all day in school without being bored all night too?

Worse, Peter's nappy baby class was coming, too. They'd probably have to be tucked in at seven o'clock, when they'd all start crying for their mamas. Ugghh. And then Miss Battle-Axe snarling at them to finish their worksheets, and Moody Margaret snoring and Anxious Andrew whimpering that he'd seen a ghost . . .

Well, no way was he going to that boring old dump without some comics to pass the time. He'd just bought the latest *Screamin' Demon* with a big article all about vampires and zombies. Yay! He couldn't wait to read it.

Perfect Peter watched him stuff his Mutant Max bag full of comics.

'Henry, you know we're not allowed to bring comics to the museum sleepover,' said Perfect Peter.

'Shut up and mind your own business, toad,' said Horrid Henry.

'Mum! Henry just called me a toad!' wailed Peter. 'And he told me to shut up.'

'Toady Toady Toady, Toady Toady Toady,' jeered Henry.

'Henry! Stop being horrid or no museum sleepover for you,' yelled Mum.

Horrid Henry paused. Was it too late to be horrid enough to get banned from the sleepover? Why hadn't he thought of this before? Why, he could . . .

'Henry! Peter! We have to leave *now!*' yelled Dad.

Rats.

The children queued up in the museum's Central Hall clutching their sleeping bags as Miss Lovely and Miss Battle-Axe ticked off names on a big register.

'Go away, Susan,' said Moody Margaret. 'After what you did at my

house I'm going to sit with Gurinder.
So there.'

'You're such a meanie, Margaret,' said
Sour Susan.

'Am not.'

'Are too.'

Susan scowled. Margaret was *always* so
mean. If only she could think of a way
to pay that old grouch back.

Margaret scowled. Susan was *always* so annoying. If only she could think of a way to pay that old fraidy cat back.

Henry scowled. Why did he have to be here? What he'd give for a magic carpet to whisk him straight home to the comfy black chair to watch *Terminator Gladiator*. Could life get any worse?

'Henwy,' came a little voice next to him. 'I love you Henwy. I want to give you a big kiss.'

Oh no, thought Horrid Henry. Oh no. It was Lisping Lily, New Nick's little sister. What was that foul fiend doing here?

'You keep away from me,' said Horrid Henry, pushing and shoving his way through the children to escape her.

'Waaa!' wept Weepy William as Henry stepped on his foot.

'I want my mama,' cried Needy Neil as Henry trampled on his sleeping bag.

'But I want to marry with you, Henwy,' lisped Lily, trying to follow him.

'Henry! Stay still!' barked Miss Battle-Axe, glaring at him with her demon eyes.

'Hello boys and girls, what an adventure we're going to have tonight,' said the museum's guide, Earnest Ella, as she handed out pencils and worksheets.

Henry groaned. Boring! He hated worksheets.

'Did you know that our museum has a famous collection of balls of wool through the ages?' droned Earnest Ella. 'And an old railway car? Oh yes, it's going to be an exciting sleepover night. We're even going on a torch-lit walk through the corridors.'

Horrid Henry yawned and sneaked a peek at his comic book, which he'd hidden beneath his museum worksheet.

Watch out, Demon Fans!! To celebrate the release of this season's big blockbuster monster horror film, **THE ZOMBIE VAMPIRES**, study this check-list. Make sure there are no zombie-vampires lurking in your neighbourhood!!!!

Horrid Henry gasped as he read *How To Recognise a Vampire* and *How to Recognise a Zombie*. Big scary teeth?

Big googly eyes? Looks like the walking dead? Wow, that described Miss Battle-Axe perfectly. All they had to add was big fat carrot nose and . . .

A dark shadow loomed over him.

'I'll take that,' snapped Miss Battle-Axe, yanking the comic out of his hand. '*And* the rest.'

Huh?

He'd been so careful. How had she spotted that comic under his worksheet?

And how did she know about the secret stash in his bag? Horrid Henry looked round the hall. Aha! There was Peter, pretending not to look at him. How dare that wormy worm toad tell on him? Just for that . . .

'Come along everyone, line up to collect your torches for our spooky walk,' said Earnest Ella. 'You wouldn't want to get left behind in the dark, would you?'

There was no time to lose. Horrid Henry slipped over to Peter's class and joined him in line with Tidy Ted and Goody Goody Gordon.

'Hello Peter,' said Henry sweetly.

Peter looked at him nervously. Did Henry suspect *he'd* told on him? Henry didn't *look* angry.

'Shame my comic got confiscated,' said Henry, ''cause it had a list of how to tell whether anyone you know is a zombie vampire.'

'A zombie vampire?' said Tidy Ted.

'Yup,' said Henry.

'They're imaginary,' said Goody-Goody Gordon.

'That's what they'd *like* you to believe,' said Henry. 'But I've discovered some.'

'Where?' said Ted.

Horrid Henry looked around dramatically, then dropped his voice to a whisper.

'Two teachers at our school,' hissed Henry.

'Two *teachers?*' said Peter.

'What?' said Ted.

'You heard me. Zombie vampires. Miss Battle-Axe *and* Miss Lovely.'

'Miss *Lovely?*' gasped Peter.

'You're just making that up,' said Gordon.

'It was all in *Screamin' Demon*,' said Henry. 'That's why Miss Battle-Axe snatched my comic. To stop me finding out the truth. Listen carefully.'

Henry recited:

'How to recognise a vampire:
1. BIG HUGE SCARY TEETH.'

'If Miss Battle-Axe's fangs were any bigger she would trip over them,' said Horrid Henry.

Tidy Ted nodded. 'She *does* have big pointy teeth.'

'That doesn't prove anything,' said Peter.

'2. DRINKS BLOOD.'

Perfect Peter shook his head. 'Drinks . . . blood?'

'*Obviously* they do, just not *in front* of people,' said Horrid Henry. 'That would give away their terrible secret.'

'3. ONLY APPEARS AT NIGHT.'

'But Henry,' said Goody-Goody Gordon, 'we see Miss Battle-Axe and Miss Lovely every day at school. They *can't* be vampires.'

Henry sighed. 'Have you been paying attention? I didn't say they were *vampires*, I said they were *zombie* vampires. Being half-zombie lets them walk about in daylight.'

Perfect Peter and Goody-Goody Gordon looked at one another.

'Here's the total proof,' Henry continued.

'How to recognise a zombie: 1. LOOKS DEAD.'

'Does Miss Battle-Axe look dead? Definitely,' said Horrid Henry. 'I never saw a more dead-looking person.'

'But Henry,' said Peter. 'She's alive.'

Unfortunately, yes, thought Horrid Henry.

'Duh,' he said. 'Zombies always *seem* alive. Plus, zombies have got scary, bulging eyes like Miss Battle-Axe,' continued Henry. 'And they feed on human flesh.'

'Miss Lovely doesn't eat human flesh,' said Peter. 'She's a vegetarian.'

'A likely story,' said Henry.

'You're just trying to scare us,' said Peter.

'Don't you see?' said Henry. 'They're planning to pounce on us during the torch-lit trail.'

'I don't believe you,' said Peter.

Henry shrugged. 'Fine. Don't believe me. Just don't say I didn't warn you when Miss Lovely lurches out of the dark and BITES you!' he shrieked.

'Be quiet, Henry,' shouted Miss Battle-Axe. 'William. Stop weeping.

There's nothing to be scared of. Linda!
Stand up. It's not bedtime yet. Bert!
Where's your torch?'

'I dunno,' said Beefy Bert.

Miss Lovely walked over and smiled
at Peter.

'Looking forward to the torchlit
walk?' she beamed.

Peter couldn't stop himself sneaking a
peek at her teeth. *Were* they big? And
sharp? Funny, he'd never noticed before
how pointy two of them were . . . And
was her face a bit . . . umm . . . pale?

No! Henry was just trying to trick
him. Well, he wasn't going to be fooled.

'Time to go exploring,' said Earnest
Ella. 'First stop on the torch-lit trail: our
brand-new exhibit, *Wonderful World of
Wool*. Then we'll be popping next door
down the *Passage to the Past* to visit the
old railway car and the Victorian shop

and a Neanderthal cave. Torches on, everyone.'

Sour Susan smiled to herself. She'd just thought of the perfect revenge on Margaret for teasing her for being such a scaredy cat.

Moody Margaret smiled to herself. She'd just thought of the perfect revenge on Susan for being so sour.

Ha ha Margaret, thought Susan. I'll get you tonight.

Ha ha Susan, thought Margaret. I'll get you tonight.

Ha ha Peter, thought Henry. I'll get you tonight.

'Follow me,' said Earnest Ella.

The children stampeded after her.

All except three.

When the coast was clear, Moody Margaret turned off her torch, darted into the pitch-black *Passage to the Past* hall and hid in the Neanderthal cave behind the caveman. She'd leap out at Susan when she walked past. MWAHAHAHAHAHAHA! Wouldn't that old scaredy cat get a fright.

Sour Susan turned off her torch and peeked down the *Passage to the Past* corridor. Empty. She tiptoed to the railway car and crept inside. Just wait till Margaret walked by . . .

Horrid Henry turned off his torch, crept down the *Passage to the Past*, sneaked into the Victorian shop and hid behind the rocking chair.

Tee hee. Just wait till Peter walked past. He'd—

What was that?

Was it his imagination? Or did that spinning wheel in the corner of the shop . . . move?

CR—EEEK went the wheel.

It was so dark. But Henry didn't dare switch on his torch.

Moody Margaret looked over from the Neanderthal cave at the Victorian shop. Was it her imagination or was that rocking chair rocking back and forth?

Sour Susan looked out from the railway car. Was it her imagination or was the caveman moving?

There was a strange, scuttling noise. What was that? thought Susan.

You know, thought Henry, this museum *is* kind of creepy at night.

And then something grabbed onto his leg.

'AAAARRRRGGHHH!' screamed
Horrid Henry.

Moody Margaret heard a blood-
curdling scream. Scarcely daring to
breathe, Margaret peeped over the
caveman's shoulder . . .

Sour Susan heard
a blood-curdling
scream. Scarcely
daring to breathe,
Susan peeped out
from the railway
carriage . . .

'Henwy, I found
you, Henwy,' piped the
creature clinging to his leg.

'Go away Lily,' hissed Henry. The
horrible fiend was going to ruin everything.

'Will you marry me, Henwy?'

'No!' said Horrid Henry, trying to shake her off and brushing against the spinning wheel.

CR—EEEEK.

The spinning wheel spun.

What's that noise? thought Margaret, craning to see from behind the caveman.

'Henwy! I want to give you a big kiss,' lisped Lily.

Horrid Henry shook his leg harder.

The spinning wheel tottered and fell over.

CRASH!

Margaret and Susan saw something lurch out of the Victorian shop and loom up in the darkness. A monstrous creature with four legs and waving arms . . .

'AAAARRRRGGHH!' screamed Susan.

'AAAARGGHHHHH!' shrieked Margaret.

'AAAARGGHHHHH!' shrieked Henry.

The unearthly screams rang through the museum. Peter, Ted, and Gordon froze.

'You don't think—' gasped Gordon.

'Not . . . ' trembled Peter.

'Zombie vampires?' whimpered Ted. They clutched one another.

'Everyone head back to the Central Hall NOW!' shouted Earnest Ella.

★

In the cafeteria, Miss Lovely and Miss Battle-Axe were snatching a short break to enjoy a lovely fried egg sandwich with lashings of ketchup.

Oh my weary bones, thought Miss Battle-Axe, as she sank her teeth into the huge sandwich. Peace at last.

AAARRGGHH! EEEEEKKK! HELLLP!

Miss Battle-Axe and Miss Lovely squeezed their sandwiches in shock as they heard the terrible screams.

SPLAT!

A stream of ketchup squirted Miss Lovely in the eye and dripped down her face onto her blouse.

SQUIRT!

A blob of ketchup splatted Miss Battle-Axe on the nose and dribbled down her chin onto her cardigan.

'Sorry, Boudicca,' said Miss Lovely.

'Sorry, Lydia,' said Miss Battle-Axe.

They raced into the dark Central Hall just as their classes ran back from the torch-lit walk. Fifty beams of light from fifty torches lit up the teachers' ketchup-covered faces and ketchup-stained clothes.

'AAAARRGGHHH!' screamed Perfect Peter.

'It's the zombie vampires!' howled Tidy Ted.

'Run for your lives!' yelped Goody-Goody Gordon.

'Wait!' shouted Miss Lovely! 'Children, come back!'

'We won't eat you!' shouted Miss Battle-Axe.

'AAAARRRRGGHHHHHH!'

ACKNOWLEDGEMENTS

Jenny Gyertson has had her lovely story
Fairies Paint the Rainbow *stolen*
not once but twice: the least she deserves
is an acknowledgement.

My thanks also to Steven Butler
for telling me all about Theft Number One . . .

HORRiD HENRY'S
Monster Movie

For Emily Lethbridge

CONTENTS

1

HORRiD HENRY'S MONSTER MOVIE

Horrid Henry loved scary movies.
He loved nothing more than curling
up on the comfy black chair with a
huge bag of popcorn and a Fizzywizz
drink, and jumping out of his seat in
shock every few minutes. He loved
wailing ghosts, oozing swamps, and
bloodthirsty monsters. No film was too
scary or too creepy for Horrid Henry.
MWAHAHAHAHAHAHA!

Perfect Peter hated scary movies. He
hated nothing more than hiding behind

the comfy black chair covering his eyes and jumping out of his skin in shock every few seconds. He hated ghosts and swamps and monsters. Even Santa Claus saying 'ho ho ho' too loudly scared him.

Thanks to Peter being the biggest scaredy-cat who ever lived, Mum and Dad would never take Henry to see any scary films.

And now, the scariest, most frightening, most terrible film ever was in town. Horrid Henry was desperate to see it.

'You're not seeing that film and that's final,' said Mum.

'Absolutely no way,' said Dad. 'Far too scary.'

'But I love scary movies!' shrieked Horrid Henry.

'I don't,' said Mum.

'I don't,' said Dad.

'I hate scary movies,' said Perfect Peter. 'Please can we see *The Big Bunny Caper* instead?'

'NO!' shrieked Horrid Henry.

'Stop shouting, Henry,' said Mum.

'But everyone's seen *The Vampire Zombie Werewolf*,' moaned Horrid Henry. 'Everyone but me.'

Moody Margaret had seen it, and said it was the best horror film ever.

Fiery Fiona had seen it three times. 'And I'm seeing it three more times,' she squealed.

Rude Ralph said he'd run screaming from the cinema.

AAAARRRRGGGGHHHHHH.

Horrid Henry thought he would explode he wanted to see *The Vampire Zombie Werewolf* so much. But no. The film came and went, and Horrid Henry wailed and gnashed.

So he couldn't believe his luck when Rude Ralph came up to him one day at playtime and said:

'I've got *The Vampire Zombie*

Werewolf film on DVD. Want to come over and watch it after school?'

Did he ever!

Horrid Henry squeezed onto the sofa between Rude Ralph and Brainy Brian. Dizzy Dave sat on the floor next to Jolly Josh and Aerobic Al. Anxious Andrew sat on a chair. He'd already covered his face with his hands. Even Moody Margaret and Sour Susan were there, squabbling over who got to sit in the armchair and who had to sit on the floor.

'OK everyone, this is it,' said Rude Ralph. 'The scariest film ever. Are we ready?'

'Yeah!'

Horrid Henry gripped the sofa as the eerie piano music started.

There was a deep, dark forest.

'I'm scared!' wailed Anxious Andrew.

'Nothing's happened yet,' said Horrid Henry.

A boy and a girl ran through the shivery, shadowy trees.

'Is it safe to look?' gasped Anxious Andrew.

'Shhh,' said Moody Margaret.

'You shhh!' said Horrid Henry.

'MWAHAAAAHAAAAHAHAHAA!' bellowed Dizzy Dave.

'I'm scared!' shrieked Anxious Andrew.

'Shut up!' shouted Rude Ralph.

The pale girl stopped running and turned to the bandaged boy.

'I can't kiss you or I'll turn into a zombie,' sulked the girl.

'I can't kiss *you* or *I'll* turn into a vampire,' scowled the boy.

'But our love is so strong!' wailed the vampire girl and the zombie boy.

'Not as strong as me!' howled the werewolf, leaping out from behind a tree stump.

'AAAAAAAARRRRGGGHHH!' screeched Anxious Andrew.

'SHUT UP!' shouted Henry and Ralph.

'Leave her alone, you walking bandage,' said the werewolf.

'Leave him alone, you smelly fur ball,' said the vampire.

'This isn't scary,' said Horrid Henry.

'Shh,' said Margaret.

'Go away!' shouted the zombie.

'You go away, you big meanie,' snarled the werewolf.

'Don't you know that two's company and three's a crowd?' hissed the vampire.

'I challenge you both to an arm-wrestling contest,' howled the werewolf. 'The winner gets to keep the arms.'

'Or in your case the paws,' sniffed the vampire.

'This is the worst film I've ever seen,' said Horrid Henry.

'Shut up, Henry,' said Margaret.

'We're trying to watch,' said Susan.

'Ralph, I thought you said this was a really scary film,' hissed Henry. 'Have you *actually* seen it before?'

Rude Ralph looked at the floor.

'No,' admitted Ralph. 'But everyone said they'd seen it and I didn't want to be left out.'

'Margaret's a big fat liar too,' said Susan. 'She never saw it either.'

'Shut up, Susan!' shrieked Margaret.

'Awhooooooo,' howled the werewolf.

Horrid Henry was disgusted. He could make a *much* scarier film. In fact . . . what was stopping him? Who better to make the scariest film of all time than

Henry? How hard could it be to make a film? You just pointed a camera and yelled, 'Action!' Then he'd be rich rich rich. He'd need a spare house just to stash all his cash. And he'd be famous, too. Everyone would be begging for a role in one of his mega-horror blockbusters. *Please can we be in your new monster film?* Mum and Dad and Peter would beg. Well, they could beg as long as they liked. He'd give them his autograph, but that would be *it*.

Henry could see the poster now:

HENRY PRODUCTIONS
PRESENT:

**THE UNDEAD
DEMON MONSTER
WHO WOULD
NOT DIE**

Starring HENRY as The Monster

Written and Filmed and Directed by
HENRY

'I could make a *really* scary film,' said
Henry.

'Not as scary as the film *I* could make,'
said Margaret.

'Ha!' said Henry. 'Your scary film wouldn't scare a toddler.'

'Ha!' said Margaret. *'Your* scary film would make a baby laugh.'

'Oh yeah?' said Henry.

'Yeah,' said Margaret.

'Well, we'll just see about that,' said Henry.

Horrid Henry walked around his garden, clutching Mum's camcorder. He could turn the garden into a swamp . . . flood a few flower beds . . . rip up the lawn and throw buckets of mud at the windows as the monster squelched his monstrous way through the undergrowth, growling and devouring, biting and—

'Henry, can I be in your movie?' said Peter.

'No,' said Henry. 'I'm making a scary

monster film. No nappy babies.'

'I am not a nappy baby,' said Peter.

'Are too.'

'Am not. Mum! Henry won't let me be in his film.'

'Henry!' yelled Mum. 'Let Peter be in your film or you can't borrow the camcorder.'

Gah! Why did everyone always get in his way? How could Henry be a great director if other people told him who to put in his film?

'Okay Peter,' said Henry, scowling. 'You can be Best Boy.'

Best Boy! That sounded super. Wow. That was a lot better than Peter had hoped.

'Best Boy!' shouted Horrid Henry. 'Get the snack table ready.'

'*Snack* table?' said Peter.

'Setting up the snack table is the most important part of making a movie,' said Henry. 'So I want biscuits and crisps and

Fizzywizz drinks – NOW!' he bellowed. 'It's hungry work making a film.'

Film-making next door at Moody Margaret's house was also proceeding slowly.

'How come I have to move the furniture?' said Susan. 'You said I could *be* in your movie.'

'Because *I'm* the director,' said Margaret. 'So *I* decide.'

'Margaret, you can be the monster in *my* film. No need for any make-up,' shouted Horrid Henry over the wall.

'Shut up, Henry,' said Margaret. 'Susan. Start walking down the path.'

'BOOOOOOOOOOOOO,' shouted Horrid Henry. 'BOOOOOOOOOOOOO.'

'Cut!' yelled Margaret. 'Quiet!' she screamed. 'I'm making a movie here.'

★

'Peter, hold the torch and shine the spotlight on me,' ordered Henry.

'Hold the torch?' said Peter.

'It's very important,' said Henry.

'Mum said you had to let me *be* in your movie,' said Peter. 'Or I'm telling on you.'

Horrid Henry glared at Perfect Peter.

Perfect Peter glared at Horrid Henry.

'Mum!' screamed Peter.

'Okay, you can be in the movie,' said Henry.

'Stop being horrid, Henry,' shouted Mum. 'Or you hand back that camera instantly.'

'I'm not being horrid; that's in the movie,' lied Henry.

Perfect Peter opened his mouth and then closed it.

'So what's my part?' said Peter.

★

Perfect Peter stood on the bench in the front garden.

'Now say your line, "I am too horrible to live," and jump off the bench into the crocodile-filled moat, where you are eaten alive and drown,' said Henry.

'I don't want to say that,' said Peter.

Horrid Henry lowered the camera. 'Do you want to be in the film or don't you?' he hissed.

'I am too horrible to live,' muttered Peter.

'Louder!' said Henry.

'I am too horrible to live,' said Peter, a fraction louder.

'And as you drown, scream out, "and I have smelly pants",' said Henry.

'*What*?' said Peter.

Tee hee, thought Horrid Henry.

'But how come you get to play all the other parts, *and* dance, *and* sing, and all I get to do is walk about going

wooooooo?' said Susan sourly in next
door's garden.

'Because it's *my* movie,' said Margaret.

'Keep it down, we're filming here,'
said Henry. 'Now Peter, you are
walking down the garden path out into
the street—'

'I thought I'd just drowned,' said
Peter.

Henry rolled his eyes.

'No dummy, this is a horror film.
You *rose* from the dead, and now you're
walking down the path singing this song,
just before the hairy scary monster leaps
out of the bushes and rips you to shreds.

'Wibble bibble dribble pants
Bibble baby wibble pants
Wibble pants wibble pants
Dribble dribble dribble pants,'

sang Horrid Henry.

Perfect Peter hesitated. 'But Henry, why would my character sing that song?'

Henry glared at Peter.

'Because I'm the director and I say so,' said Henry.

Perfect Peter's lip trembled. He started walking.

'Wibble bibble dribble pants
Bibble baby wibble pants
Wibble pants wib–'

'I don't want to!' came a screech from next door's front garden.

'Susan, you *have* to be covered up in a sheet,' said Margaret.

'But no one will see my face and know it's me,' said Susan.

'Duh,' said Margaret. 'You're playing a ghost.'

Sour Susan flung off the sheet.

'Well I quit,' said Susan.

'You're fired!' shouted Margaret.

'I don't want to sing that dribble pants song,' said Peter.

'Then you're fired!' screamed Henry.

'No!' screamed Perfect Peter. 'I quit.' And he ran out of the front garden gate, shrieking and wailing.

Wow, thought Horrid Henry. He chased after Peter, filming.

'I've had it!' screamed Sour Susan. 'I don't want to be in your stupid film!'

She ran off down the road, shrieking and wailing.

Margaret chased after her, filming.

Cool, thought Horrid Henry, what a perfect end for his film, the puny wimp running off terrified—

BUMP!

Susan and Peter collided and sprawled flat on the pavement.

CRASH!

Henry and Margaret tripped over the screaming Peter and Susan.

SMASH!

Horrid Henry dropped his camcorder.

SMASH!

Moody Margaret dropped *her* camcorder.

OOPS.

Horrid Henry stared down at the twisted broken metal as his monster movie lay shattered on the concrete path.

WHOOPS.

Moody Margaret stared down at the cracked camcorder as her Hollywood horror film lay in pieces on the ground.

'Henry!' hissed Margaret.

'Margaret!' hissed Henry.

'This is all your fault!' they wailed.

2

HORRiD HENRY'S HORRiD WEEKEND

'NOOOOOOOOO!' screamed Horrid
Henry. 'I don't want to spend the
weekend with Steve.'

'Don't be horrid, Henry,' said Mum.
'It's very kind of Aunt Ruby to invite us
down for the weekend.'

'But I hate Aunt Ruby!' shrieked
Henry. 'And I hate Steve and I hate you!'

'I can't wait to go,' said Perfect Peter.

'Shut up, Peter!' howled Henry.

'Don't tell your brother to shut up,'
shouted Mum.

'Shut up! Shut up! Shut up!' And
Horrid Henry fell to the floor wailing
and screaming and kicking.

Stuck-Up Steve was Horrid Henry's
hideous cousin. Steve hated Henry.
Henry hated him. The last time Henry
had seen Steve, Henry had tricked
him into thinking there was a monster
under his bed. Steve had sworn revenge.
Then there was the other time at the
restaurant when . . . well, Horrid Henry
thought it would be a good idea to
avoid Steve until his cousin was grown-
up and in prison for crimes against
humanity.

And now his mean, horrible parents were forcing him to spend a whole precious weekend with the toadiest, wormiest, smelliest boy who ever slimed out of a swamp.

Mum sighed. 'We're going and that's that. Ruby says Steve is having a lovely friend over so that should be extra fun.'

Henry stopped screaming and kicking. Maybe Steve's friend wouldn't be a stuck-up monster. Maybe *he'd* been forced to waste his weekend with Steve, too. After all, who'd volunteer to spend time with Steve? Maybe together they could squish Stuck-Up Steve once and for all.

Ding dong.

Horrid Henry, Perfect Peter, Mum and Dad stood outside Rich Aunt Ruby's enormous house on a grey, drizzly day. Steve opened the massive front door.

'Oh,' he sneered. 'It's you.'

Steve opened the present Mum had brought. It was a small flashlight. Steve put it down.

'I already have a much better one,' he said.

'Oh,' said Mum.

Another boy stood beside him. A boy who looked vaguely familiar. A boy . . . Horrid Henry gasped. Oh no. It was Bill. Bossy Bill. The horrible son of Dad's boss. Henry had once tricked Bill into photocopying his bottom. Bill had sworn revenge. Horrid Henry's insides turned to jelly. Trust Stuck-Up Steve to be friends with Bossy Bill. It was bad enough being trapped in a house with one Arch-Enemy. Now he was stuck in a house with TWO . . .

Stuck-up Steve scowled at Henry. 'You're wearing that old shirt of mine,' he said. 'Don't your parents ever buy you new clothes?'

Bossy Bill snorted.

'Steve,' said Aunt Ruby. 'Don't be rude.'

'I wasn't,' said Steve. 'I was just asking. No harm in asking, is there?'

'No,' said Horrid Henry. He smiled at Steve. 'So when will Aunt Ruby buy you a new face?'

'Henry,' said Mum. 'Don't be rude.'

'I was just asking,' said Henry. 'No harm in asking, is there?' he added, glaring at Steve.

Steve glared back.

Aunt Ruby beamed. 'Henry, Steve and Bill are taking you to their friend Tim's paintballing party.'

'Won't that be fun,' said Mum.

Peter looked frightened.

'Don't worry, Peter,' said Aunt Ruby, 'you can help me plant seedlings while the older boys are out.'

Peter beamed. 'Thank you,' he said. 'I don't like paintballing. Too messy and scary.'

Paintballing! Horrid Henry loved paintballing. The chance to splat Steve and Bill with ooey gooey globs of paint . . . hmmm, maybe the weekend was looking up.

'Great!' said Horrid Henry.

'How nice,' said Rich Aunt Ruby,
'you boys already know each other.
Think how much fun you're all going to
have sharing Steve's bedroom together.'

Uh-oh, thought Horrid Henry.

'Yeah!' said Stuck-Up Steve. 'We're
looking forward to sharing a room with
Henry.' His piggy eyes gleamed.

'Yeah!' said Bossy Bill. 'I can't wait.'
His piggy eyes gleamed.

'Yeah,' said Horrid Henry. He wouldn't be sleeping a wink.

Horrid Henry looked around the enormous high-ceilinged bedroom he'd be sharing with his two evil enemies for two very long days and one very long night. There was a bunk-bed, which Steve and Bill had already nabbed, and two single beds. Steve's bedroom shelves were stuffed with zillions of new toys and games, as usual.

Bill and Steve smirked at each other. Henry scowled at them. What were they plotting?

'Don't you dare touch my Super-Blooper Blaster,' said Steve.

'Don't you dare touch my Demon Dagger Sabre,' said Bill.

A Super-Blooper Blaster! A Demon Dagger Sabre! Trust Bill and Steve to

have the two best toys in the world . . .
Rats.

'Don't worry,' said Henry. 'I don't
play with baby toys.'

'Oh yeah,' said Stuck-Up Steve. 'Bet
you're too much of a baby to jump off
my top bunk onto your bed.'

'Am not,' said Henry.

'We're not allowed to jump on beds,'
said Perfect Peter.

'We're not allowed,' mimicked Steve.
'I thought you were too poor to even
have beds.'

'Ha ha,' said Henry.

'Chicken. Chicken. Scaredy cat,'
sneered Bossy Bill.

'Squawk!' said Stuck-Up Steve. 'I
knew you'd be too scared, chicken.'

That did it. *No* one called Horrid
Henry chicken and lived. As if he,
Henry, leader of a pirate gang, would be

afraid to jump off a top bunk. Ha.

'Don't do it, Henry,' said Perfect
Peter.

'Shut up, worm,' said Henry.

'But it's so high,' squealed Peter,
squeezing his eyes shut.

Horrid Henry clambered up the ladder and stepped onto the top bunk. 'It's nothing,' he lied. 'I've jumped off MUCH higher.'

'Well, go on then,' said Stuck-Up Steve.

Boing! Horrid Henry bounced.

Boing! Horrid Henry bounced higher. Whee! This bed was very springy.

'We're waiting, chicken,' said Bossy Bill.

BOING! BOING! Horrid Henry bent his knees, then – – – leap! He jumped onto the single bed below.

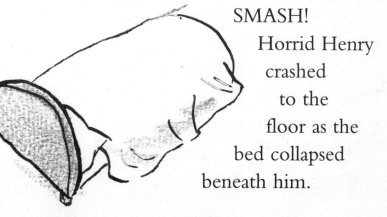

SMASH! Horrid Henry crashed to the floor as the bed collapsed beneath him.

Huh? What? How could he have broken the bed? He hadn't heard any breaking sounds.

It was as if . . . as if . . .

Mum, Dad and Aunt Ruby ran into the room.

'Henry broke the bed,' said Stuck-Up Steve.

'We tried to stop him,' said Bossy Bill, 'but Henry insisted on jumping.'

'But . . . but . . .' said Horrid Henry.

'Henry!' wailed Mum. 'You horrid boy.'

'How could you be so horrid?' said Dad. 'No pocket money for a year. Ruby, I'm so sorry.'

Aunt Ruby pursed her lips. 'These things happen,' she said.

'And no paintballing party for you,' said Mum.

What?

'No!' wailed Henry.

Then Horrid Henry saw a horrible sight. Behind Aunt Ruby's back, Steve and Bill were covering their mouths and laughing. Henry realised the terrible truth. Bill and Steve had tricked him.

They'd broken the bed. And now *he'd* got the blame.

'But I didn't break it!' screamed Henry.

'Yes you did, Henry,' said Peter. 'I saw you.'

AAAARRRRGGGGHHHH! Horrid Henry leapt at Peter. He was a storm god hurling thunderbolts at a foolish mortal.

'AAAIIIEEEEEE!' squealed Perfect Peter.

'Henry! Stop it!' shrieked Mum. 'Leave your brother alone.'

Nah nah ne nah nah mouthed Steve behind Aunt Ruby's back.

'Isn't it lovely how nicely the boys are playing together?' said Aunt Ruby.

'Yes, isn't it?' said Mum.

'Not surprising,' said Aunt Ruby, beaming. 'After all, Steve is such a polite, friendly boy, I've never met anyone who didn't love him.'

Snore! Snore! Snore!

Horrid Henry lay on a mattress listening to hideous snoring sounds. He'd stayed awake for hours, just in case they tried anything horrible, like

pouring water on his head, or stuffing
frogs in his bed. Which was what he was
going to do to Peter, the moment he
got home.

Henry had just spent the most horrible
Saturday of his life. He'd begged to go to
the paintballing party. He'd pleaded to go
to the paintballing party. He'd screamed
about going to the paintballing party. But
no. His mean, horrible parents wouldn't
budge. And it was all Steve and Bill's fault.
They'd tripped him going down the stairs.

They'd kicked him under the table at dinner (and then complained that he was kicking *them*). And every time Aunt Ruby's back was turned they stuck out their tongues and jeered: 'We're going paintballing, and you're not.'

He had to get to that party. And he had to be revenged. But how? How? His two Arch-Enemies had banded together and struck the first blow. Could he booby-trap their beds and remove a few slats? Unfortunately, everyone would know *he'd* done it and he'd be in even more trouble than he was now.

Scare them? Tell them there was a monster under the bed? Hmmm. He knew Steve was as big a scaredy cat as Peter. But he'd already done that once. He didn't think Steve would fall for it again.

Get them into trouble? Turn them
against each other? Steal their best
toys and hide them? Hmmm. Hmmm.
Horrid Henry thought and thought.
He had to be revenged. He had to.

Tweet tweet. It was Sunday morning.
The birds were singing. The sun was
shining. The—

Yank!

Bossy Bill and Stuck-Up Steve pulled
off his duvet.

'Nah na ne nah nah, we-ee beat you,'
crowed Bill.

'Nah na ne nah nah, we got you into
trouble,' crowed Steve.

Horrid Henry scowled. Time to put
Operation Revenge into action.

'Bill thinks you're bossy, Steve,' said
Henry. 'He told me.'

'Didn't,' said Bossy Bill.

'And Steve thinks you're stuck-up, Bill,' added Henry sweetly.

'No I don't,' said Steve.

'Then why'd you tell me that?' said Horrid Henry.

Steve stuck his nose in the air. 'Nice try Henry, you big loser,' said Stuck-Up Steve. 'Just ignore him, Bill.'

'Henry, it's not nice to tell lies,' said Perfect Peter.

'Shut up, worm,' snarled Horrid Henry.

Rats.

Time for plan B.

Except he didn't have a plan B.

'I can't wait for Tim's party,' said Bossy Bill. 'You never know what's going to happen.'

'Yeah, remember when he told us he was having a pirate party and instead we went to the Wild West Theme Park!' said Steve.

'Or when he said we were having a sleepover, and instead we all went to a Manic Buzzards concert.'

'And Tim gives the best party bags. Last year everyone got a Deluxe Demon Dagger Sabre,' said Steve. 'Wonder what he'll give this year? Oh, I forgot, Henry won't be coming to the party.'

'Too bad you can't come, Henry,' sneered Bossy Bill.

'Yeah, too bad,' sneered Stuck-Up Steve. 'Not.'

ARRRRGGGHH. Horrid Henry's blood boiled. He couldn't decide what was worse, listening to them crow about having got him into so much trouble, or brag about the great party they were going to and he wasn't.

'I can't wait to find out what surprises he'll have in store this year,' said Bill.

'Yeah,' said Steve.

Who cares? thought Horrid Henry.
Unless Tim was planning to throw Bill
and Steve into a shark tank. That would
be a nice surprise. Unless of course . . .

And then suddenly Horrid Henry had a brilliant, spectacular idea. It was so brilliant, and so spectacular, that for a moment he wondered whether he could stop himself from flinging open the window and shouting his plan out loud. Oh wow. Oh wow. It was risky. It was dangerous. But if it worked, he would have the best revenge ever in the history of the world. No, the history of the solar system. No, the history of the universe!

It was an hour before the party. Horrid Henry was counting the seconds until he could escape.

Aunt Ruby popped her head round the door waving an envelope.

'Letter for you boys,' she said.

Steve snatched it and tore it open.

Dear Steve and Bill

Party of the year update.
Everyone must come to my house
wearing pyjamas (you'll find
out why later, but don't be
surprised if we all end up in
a film—shhhhh). It'll be a real
laugh. Make sure to bring
your favourite soft toys, too,
and wear your fluffiest
slippers. Hollywood, here
we come!

Tim

'He must be planning something
amazing,' said Bill.

'I bet we're all going to be acting in a

film!' said Steve.

'Yeah!' said Bill.

'Too bad *you* won't, Henry,' said Stuck-Up Steve.

'You're so lucky,' said Henry. 'I wish I were going.'

Mum looked at Dad.

Dad looked at Mum.

Henry held his breath.

'Well, you can't, Henry, and that's final,' said Mum.

'It's so unfair!' shrieked Henry.

Henry's parents dropped Steve and Bill off at Tim's party on their way home. Steve was in his blue bunny pyjamas and blue bunny fluffy slippers, and clutching a panda.

Bill was in his yellow duckling pyjamas and yellow duckling fluffy slippers, and clutching his monkey.

'Shame you can't come, Henry,' said Steve, smirking. 'But we'll be sure to tell you all about it.'

'Do,' said Henry, as Mum drove off.

Horrid Henry heard squeals of laughter at Hoity-Toity Tim's front door. Bill and Steve stood frozen. Then they started to wave frantically at the car.

'Are they saying something?' said
Mum, glancing in the rear-view mirror.

'Nah, just waving goodbye,' said
Horrid Henry. He rolled down his
window.

'Have fun, guys!'

3

HORRID HENRY'S GRUMP CARD

'I've been so good!' shrieked Horrid
Henry. 'Why can't I have a grump card?'

'You have not been good,' said Mum.

'You've been awful,' said Dad.

'No I haven't,' said Henry.

Mum sighed. 'Just today you pinched
Peter and called him names. You
pushed him off the comfy black chair.
You screamed. You wouldn't eat your
sprouts. You—'

'Aside from *that*,' said Horrid Henry.
'I've been *so* good. I deserve a grump card.'

'Henry,' said Dad. 'You know we only give grump cards for *exceptionally* good behaviour.'

'But I never get one!' howled Henry.

Mum and Dad looked at each other.

'And why do you think that is?' said Mum.

'Because you're mean and unfair and the worst parents in the world!' screamed Horrid Henry.

What other reason could there be?

A grump card was precious beyond gold and silver and rubies and diamonds. If Mum or Dad thought you'd behaved totally brilliantly above and beyond the call of duty they gave you a grump card. A grump card meant that you could erase any future punishment. A grump card was a glittering, golden, get-out-of-jail-free ticket.

Horrid Henry had never had a grump

card. Just think, if he had even one . . . if Dad was in the middle of telling him off, or banning him from the computer for a week, all Henry had to do was hand him a grump card, and, like magic, the telling off would end, the punishment would be erased, and Henry would be back on the computer zapping baddies.

Horrid Henry longed for a grump card. But how could he ever get one?

Even Peter, who was always perfect,
only had seven. And he'd never even
used a single one. What a waste. What a
total waste.

Imagine what he could do if he had
a grump card . . . He could scoff every
sweet and biscuit and treat in the house.
He could forget all about homework
and watch telly instead. And best of all,
if Dad ever tried to ban him from the
computer, or Mum shouted that he'd
lost his pocket money for a month, all
Henry had to do was produce the magic
card.

What bliss.

What heaven.

What joy.

But *how* could Henry get a grump
card? How? How?

Could he behave totally brilliantly
above and beyond the call of duty?

Horrid Henry considered. Nah. That was impossible. He'd once spent a whole day being perfect, and even then had ended up being sent to his room.

So how else to get a grump card?

Steal one? Hmmm. Tempting. Very tempting. He could sneak into Peter's room, snatch a grump card or two, then sneak out again. He could even substitute a fake grump card at the bottom in case Peter noticed his stash

was smaller. But then Peter would
be sure to tell on him when Henry
produced the golden ticket to freedom,
and Mum and Dad would be so cross
they'd probably *double* his punishment
and ban him from the computer
for life.

Or, he could kidnap Fluff Puff, Peter's
favourite plastic sheep, and hold

him for ransom. Yes!
And then when Peter
had ransomed him back,
Henry could steal him
again. And again. Until
all Peter's grump cards

were his. Yes! He was brilliant. He was
a genius. Why had he never thought of
this before?

Except . . . if Peter told on him,
Henry had a horrible feeling that he
would get into trouble. Big big trouble

that not even a grump card could get him out of.

Time to think again. Could he swap something for one? What did Henry have that Peter wanted? Comics? No. Crisps? No. Killer Boy Rats CDs? No way.

Henry sighed. Maybe he could *buy* one from Peter. Unfortunately, Horrid Henry never had any money. Whatever pitiful pocket money he ever had always seemed to vanish through his fingers. Besides, who'd want to give that wormy worm a penny?

Better yet, could Henry *trick* Peter into giving him one? Yeah! They could play a great game called *Learn to Share*. Henry could tell Peter to give him half his grump cards as Peter needed to learn to stop being such a selfish hog. It *could* work . . .

There was a snuffling sound, like a pig rustling for truffles, and Perfect Peter stuck his head round the door.

'What are you doing, Henry?' asked Peter.

'None of your business,

worm,' said Horrid Henry.

'Want to play with me?' said Peter.

'No,' said Henry. Peter was always nagging Henry to play with him. But when Henry *had* played Robot and Mad Professor with him, for some reason Peter hadn't enjoyed giving Henry all his sweets and money and doing all Henry's chores for him.

'We could play checkers . . . or Scrabble?' said Peter.

'N-O spells no,' said Henry. 'Now get out of—' Horrid Henry paused. Wait a minute. Wait a minute . . .

'How much will you pay me?' said Horrid Henry.

Perfect Peter stared at Henry.

'Pay you? *Pay* you to play with me?'

'Yeah,' said Henry.

Perfect Peter considered.

'How much?' said Peter slowly.

'One pound a minute,' said Henry.

'One pound a minute!' said Peter.

'It's a good offer, toad,' said Henry.

'No it isn't,' said Peter.

'What, you think it should be two pounds a minute?' said Henry. 'Okay.'

'I'm going to tell on you,' said Peter.

'Tell what, worm? That I made you a perfectly good offer? No one's forcing you.'

Perfect Peter paused. Henry was right. He could just say no.

'Or . . .' said Horrid Henry. 'You could pay me in grump cards.'

272

'Grump cards?' said Peter.

'After all, you have tons and you never use them,' said Henry. 'You could spare one or two or four and never notice . . . and you'll refill your stash in no time.'

It was true that he didn't really need his grump cards, thought Peter. And it would be so nice to play a game . . .

'Okay,' said Peter.

YES! thought Horrid Henry. What a genius he was.

'I charge one grump card a minute.'

'No,' said Peter. 'Grump cards are valuable.'

Horrid Henry sighed.

'Tell you what, because I'm such a nice brother, I will play you a game of Scra . . . Scrab . . .' Horrid Henry could barely bring himself to even say the word *Scrabble* . . . 'for two grump cards. And a game of checkers for two more.'

'And a soft toy tea party?' said Peter. Did anyone suffer as much as Henry? He sighed, loudly.

'Okay,' said Horrid Henry. 'But that'll cost you three.'

Horrid Henry stared happily at his seven glorious grump cards. He'd done it! He was free to do anything he wanted. He would be king for ever.

Why wait?

Horrid Henry skipped downstairs, went straight to the sweet jar, and took a huge handful of sweets.

'Put those back, Henry,' said Mum. 'You know sweet day is Saturday.'

'Don't care,' said Henry. 'I want sweets now and I'm having them now.' Shoving the huge handful into his mouth, he reached into the jar for more.

'Henry!' screamed Mum. 'Put those back. That's it. No sweets for a week. Now go straight—'

Horrid Henry whipped out a grump card and handed it to Mum.

Mum gasped. Her jaw dropped.

'Where . . . when . . . did you get a grump card?'

Henry shrugged. 'I got it 'cause I was so good.'

Mum stared at him. Dad must have given him one. How amazing.

Henry strolled into the sitting room. Time for *Terminator Gladiator*!

Dad was sitting on the sofa watching the boring news. Well, not for long. Horrid Henry grabbed the clicker and switched channels.

'Hey,' said Dad. 'I was watching.'

'Tough,' said Henry. 'I'm watching what I want to watch. Go Gladiator!' he squealed.

'Don't be horrid, Henry. I'm warning you . . .'

Horrid Henry stuck out his tongue at
Dad. 'Buzz off, baldie.'

Dad gasped.

'That's it, Henry. No computer games
for a week. Now go straight—'

Dad stared at the grump card which
Henry waved at him. Henry? A grump
card? Mum must have given him one.
But how? When?

'I'll just go off now and play on the
computer,' said Henry, smirking.

Tee hee. The look on Dad's face. And
what fun to play on the computer, after
he'd been banned from it! That was well

worth a grump card. After all, he had plenty.

Horrid Henry spat his sprouts onto the floor. But a grump card took care of the 'no TV for the rest of the day' punishment. Then he flicked peas at Peter and nicked four of his chips. That was well worth a grump card, too, thought Horrid Henry, to get his pocket money back. Bit of a shame that he had to give two grump cards to lift the ban on going to Ralph's sleepover, but, hey, that's what grump cards were for, right?

'Henry, it's my turn to play on the computer,' said Peter.

'Tough,' said Horrid Henry, zapping and blasting.

'I'm going to tell on you,' said Peter.

'Go ahead,' said Henry. 'See if I care.'

'You're going to get into big, big trouble,' said Peter.

'Go away, wormy worm toady pants poopsicle,' said Henry. 'You're annoying me.'

'Mum! Henry just called me a wormy worm toady pants poopsicle!' shrieked Peter.

'Henry! Stop calling your brother names,' said Mum.

'I didn't,' shouted Henry.

'He did too!' howled Peter.

'Shut up, Ugg-face!' snarled Henry.

'Mum! Henry just called me Ugg-face!'

'That's it,' said Mum. 'Henry! Go to your room. No computer for a—'

Horrid Henry handed over another grump card.

'Henry. Where did you get these?' said
Mum.

'I was given them for being good,' said
Horrid Henry. That wasn't a lie, because
he *had* been good by playing with Peter,
and Peter had given them to him.

Perfect Peter burst into tears.

'Henry tricked me,' said Peter. 'He
took my grump cards.'

'Didn't.'

'Did.'

'We made a deal, you wibble-face
nappy!' shrieked Henry, and attacked.
He was a bulldozer flattening a wriggling
worm . . .

'AAARRRGGGHH!' screamed Peter.

'You horrid boy,' said Mum. 'No
pocket money for a week. No TV for
a week. No computer for a week. No
sweets for a week. Go to your room!'

Whoa, grump card to the rescue.
Thank goodness he'd saved one for
emergencies.

What? Huh?

Horrid Henry felt frantically inside his pockets. He looked on the floor. He checked his pockets again. And again.

There were no grump cards left.

What had he done? Had he just blown all his grump cards in an hour? His precious, precious grump cards?

The grump cards he'd never, ever get again?

NOOOOOOOOO!!!!!!!

4

HORRiD HENRY'S OLYMPICS

Chomp chomp chomp chomp . . .
Burp.

Ahhh! Horrid Henry scoffed the last
crumb of Super Spicy Hedgehog crisps
and burped again. So yummy. Wow.
He'd eaten the entire pack in seventeen
seconds. No one could guzzle crisps
faster than Horrid Henry, especially
when he was having to gobble them
secretly in class. He'd never been caught,
not even—

A dark, icy shadow fell across him.

'Are you eating in class, Henry?' hissed Miss Battle-Axe.

'No,' said Henry.

Tee hee. Thanks to his super-speedy jaws, he'd *already* swallowed the evidence.

'Then where did this crisp packet come from?' said Miss Battle-Axe, pointing to the plastic bag on the floor.

Henry shrugged.

'Bert! Is this yours?'

'I dunno,' said Beefy Bert.

'There is *no* eating in class,' said Miss Battle-Axe. Why did she have to say the same things over and over? One day the Queen would discover that she, Boudicca Battle-Axe, was her long-lost daughter and sweep her off to the palace, where she would live a life of pampered luxury. But until then—

'Now, as I was saying, before I was so rudely interrupted,' she glared at Horrid

Henry, 'our school will be having its
very own Olympics. We'll be running
and jumping and swimming and—'

'Eating!' yelled Horrid Henry.

'Quiet, Henry,' snapped Miss Battle-
Axe. 'I want all of you to practise hard,
both in school and out, to show—'

Horrid Henry stopped listening. It
was so unfair. Wasn't it bad enough that
every morning he had to heave his heavy
bones out of bed to go to school, without

wasting any of his precious TV-watching time running and jumping and swimming? He was a terrible runner. He was a pathetic jumper. He was a hopeless swimmer – though he did have his five-metre badge . . . Besides, Aerobic Al was sure to win every medal. In fact they should just give them all to him now and save everyone else a load of bother.

Shame, thought Horrid Henry, that the things he was so good at never got prizes. If there was a medal for who could watch TV the longest, or who could eat the most sweets, or who was quickest out of the classroom door when the home bell rang, well, he'd be covered in gold from head to toe.

'Go on, Susan! Jump higher.'

'I'm jumping as high as I can,' said Sour Susan.

'That's not high,' said Moody Margaret. 'A tortoise could jump higher than you.'

'Then get a tortoise,' snapped Susan sourly.

'You're just a lazy lump.'

'You're just a moody meanie.'

'Lump.'

'Meanie.'

'LUMP!'

'MEANIE!'

Slap!

Slap!

'Whatcha doin'?' asked Horrid Henry, leaning over the garden wall.

'Go away, Henry,' said Margaret.

'Yeah, Henry,' said Susan.

'I can stand in my own garden if I want to,' said Henry.

'Just ignore him,' said Margaret.

'We're practising for the school Olympics,' said Susan.

Horrid Henry snorted.

'I don't see *you* practising,' said Margaret.

'That's 'cause I'm doing my *own* Olympics, frog-face,' said Henry.

His jaw dropped. YES! YES! A thousand times yes! Why hadn't he thought of this before? Of course he should set up his own Olympics.

And have the competitions he'd always wanted to have. A name-calling competition! A chocolate-eating competition! A crisp-eating competition! A who-could-watch-the-most-TVs-at-the-same-time-competition! He'd make sure he had competitions that *he* could win. The Henry Olympics. The Holympics. And the prizes would be . . . the prizes would be . . . masses and masses of chocolate!

'Can Ted and Gordon

291

and I be in your
Olympics?' said
Perfect Peter.

'NO!' said
Henry. Who'd
want some nappy
babies competing?
They'd spoil everything, they'd—

Wait a minute . . .

'Of course you can, Peter,' said Henry
smoothly. 'That will be one pound
each.'

'Why?' said Ted.

'To pay for the super fantastic
prizes, of course,' said Henry. 'Each
champion will win a massive prize of . . .
chocolate!'

Peter's face fell.

'Oh,' he said.

'And a medal,' added Henry quickly.

'Oh,' said Peter, beaming.

'How massive?' said Margaret.

'Armfuls and armfuls,' said Horrid Henry. His mouth watered just thinking about it.

'Hmmm,' said Margaret. 'Well, I think there should be a speed haircutting competition. And dancing.'

'Dancing?' said Henry. Well, why not? He was a brilliant dancer. His elephant stomp would win any competition hands down. 'Okay.'

Margaret and Susan plonked down one pound each.

'By the way, that's *ballroom* dancing,' said Margaret.

'No way,' said Henry.

'No ballroom dancing, then we won't enter,' said Margaret. 'And Linda and Gurinder and Kate and Fiona and Soraya won't either.'

Horrid Henry considered. He was sure to win everything else, so why not let her have a tiny victory? And the more people who entered, the more chocolate for him!

'Okay,' said Henry.

'Bet you're scared I'll win everything,' said Margaret.

'Am not.'

'Are too.'

'I can eat more sweets than you any day.'

'Ha!' said Margaret. 'I'd like to see you try.'

'The Purple Hand Gang can beat the Secret Club *and* the Best Boys Club, no sweat,' said Horrid Henry. 'Bring it on.'

★

THE REAL OLYMPICS ARE HERE!

TIRED OF BORING OLD SWIMMING AND RUNNING? OF COURSE YOU ARE!

NOW'S YOUR CHANCE TO COMPETE IN THE

HOLYMPICS

THE GREATEST OLYMPICS OF ALL!!!

SPEED-EATING SWEETS! TV WATCHING! CRISP EATING! BURP TO THE BEAT!

BALLROOM DANCING. SPEED HAIRCUTTING.

Entry Fee £1 for the chance to win loads of chocolate!!!!!

'Hang on,' said Margaret. 'What's with calling this the Holympics? It should be the Molympics. I came up with the haircutting and dancing competitions.'

''Cause Molympics is a terrible name,' said Henry.

'So's Holympics,' said Margaret.

'Actually,' said Peter, 'I think it should be called the Polympics.'

'Shut up, worm,' said Henry.

'Yeah, worm,' said Margaret.

'Mum!' screamed Henry. '**MUM!!!!!!!!**'

Mum came running out of the shower.

'What is it, Henry?' she said, dripping water all over the floor. 'Are you all right?'

'I need sweets,' he said.

'You got me out of the shower because you need sweets?' she repeated.

'I need to practise for the sweet speed-eating competition,' said Henry. 'For my Olympics.'

'Absolutely not,' said Mum.

Horrid Henry was outraged.

'How am I supposed to win if I can't practise?' he howled. 'You're always telling me to practise stuff. And now when I want to you won't let me.'

Bookings for Henry's Olympics were brisk. Everyone in Henry's class – and a few from Peter's – wanted to compete. Horrid Henry gazed happily at the £45 pounds' worth of chocolate and crisps piled high on his bed. Wow. Wow. Mega mega wow. Boxes and boxes and boxes filled with yummy, yummy sweets! Giant bar after giant bar of chocolate. His Holympics would have the best prizes ever. And he, Henry, fully expected to win most of them. He'd win enough chocolate to last him a lifetime AND have the glory of coming first, for once.

Horrid Henry gazed at the chocolate prize mountain.

The chocolate prize mountain gazed back at him, and winked.

Wait.

He, Henry, was doing ALL the work. Surely it was only fair if he got *something* for his valuable time. He should have

kept a bit of money
back to cover his
expenses.

Horrid Henry
removed a giant
chocolate bar from
the pile.

After all, I do need
to practise for the
speed-eating contest,
he thought, tearing
off the wrapper and

shoving a massive piece into his mouth. And then another. Oh boy, was that chocolate yummy. In a few seconds, it was gone.

Yeah! Horrid Henry, chocolate-eating champion of the universe!

You know, thought Henry, gazing at the chocolate mound teetering precariously on his bed, I think I bought *too* many prizes. And I *do* need to practise for my event . . .

What a great day, thought Horrid Henry happily. He'd won the sweet speed-eating competition (though Greedy Graham had come a close second), the crisp-eating contest AND the name-calling one. (Peter had run off screaming when Henry called him Wibble Wobble Pants, Nappy Noodle, and Odiferous.)

Rude Ralph won 'Burp to the

Beat'. Margaret and Susan won best
ballroom dancers. Vain Violet was the
surprise winner of the speed haircutting
competition. Weepy William
. . . well, his hair would grow back –
eventually.

Best of all, Aerobic Al didn't win a
thing.

The winners gathered round to collect
their prizes.

'Where's my chocolate, Henry?' said Moody Margaret.

'And there had better be loads like you promised,' said Vain Violet.

Horrid Henry reached into the big prize bag.

Now, where was the ballroom dancing prize?

He pulled out a Choco Bloco. Yikes, was that all the chocolate he had left? He rummaged around some more.

'A Choco Bloco?' said Margaret slowly. 'A *single* Choco Bloco?'

'They're very yummy,' said Henry.

'And mine?' said Violet.

'And mine?' said Ralph.

'And mine for coming second?' said Graham.

'You're meant to share it!' screamed Horrid Henry, as he turned and ran.

Wow, thought Horrid Henry, as he fled down the road, Rude Ralph, Moody Margaret, Sour Susan, Vain Violet, and Greedy Graham chasing after him, I'm pretty fast when I need to be. Maybe I *should* enter the school Olympics after all.

Acknowledgments

Thanks to Imogen Stubbs
for sharing some fine film-making
moments with me.